Also by Sofia

An Elemental Series:
Terra
Torch
Tempest
Tidal

Spinoffs:
Operation Kane, Book2.5
Operation Jewels, Book 5

Standalone:
Dream Weaver

FAE AND FLAMES
Sofia Simpson
Copyright © 2026
Published by Starlight Books
First Edition

ISBN: 979-8-9993845-4-6 (ebook)
ISBN: 979-8-9993845-6-0 (paperback)

Cover Design by: Candice Yamnitz
Editing by: Jessica Gwyn, Jake Stoddard
Illustration by: @Yukamiart (Instagram)

FAE AND FLAMES

From the Realms of Lurin

A Romantic Regency-Inspired Fantasy

Written by
SOFIA SIMPSON

Duke
& Elora

Contents

To those who wish they had a talking phoenix to spar with...keep dreaming, maybe one day she'll arrive in your dreams.

NEBRARIA
Bular
DOVIN
Daltin
Falben
Cessa
Lumiara Mountains

Chapter One

The Prince

Duke struggles to get the gear in place. He slaps it on the table and sits back, crossing his arms. "This isn't working. I might as well scrap this entire piece." The underground bunker is dim at best, so he adjusts the lantern to lend its light on his current failure. But of course, he doesn't get away with that dispirited thought.

Stop complaining and just figure it out.

He looks up and grumbles under his breath at his pet phoenix, Char. She could use a good dousing. He inches his hand toward a cup of water.

She narrows her eyes. *Don't you dare.*

Holding her gaze, he picks up the cup slowly and then takes a drink before setting it back down.

Wise choice.

Huffing, he studies his project. The large boat-like craft has the suggestion of an engine on the front, but now he has to get it to actually work. Scowling, he puts the gear in place and fumbles with a small screw to hold it fast. His large hands struggle with the dexterity required to manipulate the tiny pieces of his project. His cuffs ride up his forearms. His shirt wouldn't suggest he's a slender fae, the way it tugs on his shoulders, but it's an old one he wore when he was younger. He knows better than to risk a fine shirt being ruined with oil or grease. Chancing a maid finding it would be unacceptable. She might suspect his less than royal activities.

He's supposed to be an indolent prince after all.

The screw slips and drops to the floor. "If anything isn't measuring up to expectations, it's this stupid screw." He shakes his head to move his hair away from his eyes so he can pick up the blasted piece of metal.

You have brains. Use that wasted space inside your head to come up with a solution.

Duke rises, frowns and pushes his spectacles off his eyes, up onto his head. He only needs them to see up close. With his long hair away from his face, he can now focus his attention on his sharp-tongued friend.

"If I had encouragement, *dear Charlotte,* instead of a constant barrage of disparaging remarks, I might figure this thing out before the New Year."

Haven't you ever heard of tough love?

He holds in a sigh. She's infuriatingly correct; it's his own failing that makes him want to throw in the towel. But Char would never let him do it. She'd threaten to light up this entire lair and say she was doing him a favor and that he needed a new project anyway.

Do you need me to get you an energy crystal? Would that put some pep in your step?

"No, I'm fine," he mutters. If only goblin crystals could generate ideas. That would help.

You don't look fine.

Duke steps back to get a better view of his current problem, ignoring her observation. He blinks away the fuzzy vision from his lack of sleep and admires his work of art.

He approaches the overly large table it rests on and runs his hand over the main body of the craft. His fingers glide over the smooth wood that looks almost like a small kayak. But it only resembles a boat. The seat in the stern is deep enough that once inside, only his head will stick out. He's made the seat adjustable so anyone could fit. And his invention of a propellor that sits at the front of the engine, also gives it a distinct look. The two planks of boards will spin to help propel the plane into flight and he's inordinately proud of it.

But even the thought of his creation isn't enough to revive his spirits. He blinks to sharpen his vision.

He runs a hand over his face and slaps his cheeks to wake himself up. Appreciating his work won't get it to the finish line. He must keep going. If only he could tell that to his sleep-deprived body. He works when he can get away from his royal schedule, which isn't often. Unfortunately, he spends many of his nights entertaining the fae nobility. He has to forgo sleep to allow for this hidden activity.

Lack of sleep isn't going to help you finish this...thing of yours.

Duke huffs. "It's not a *thing*. It's the first-ever flying machine. And sometimes I really hate that you can hear what I think. Can I please have *some* thoughts to myself?"

No. She side-eyes him. *I am mind-melded to the future king of the fae. The Creator has seen fit for me to hear all your words.*

Char regards her wing. *Still ...* She preens her feathers with single-minded devotion. *Hearing your thoughts does not compare to the beauty He has bestowed on me.*

That ludicrous statement makes him reach for his oil can.

With a squawk, Char flies off to a perch further away.

He chuckles. "That was a warning."

Forcing me to bathe would only make me retaliate with my glorious fire. Your little project here would be first in my sights.

"I wouldn't do it anyway, Char, you know that." He sets down the oil can. Bothering her is bothering him.

Immersed in water ... Char shudders, and flames flicker from her tail feathers. *It's bad enough when it rains.*

Duke's happy Char has this place to go to when the weather turns, and especially so he can hide her. If their bond became public knowledge, he would land in some serious hot water. Phoenixes are outlawed in Nebraria. The Fae live in elaborate, multi-storied tree houses, all vulnerable to fire. Duke is the prince, heir to this great kingdom. His lawbreaking would be unfathomable to his subjects.

He could never give up his bond with Char, though. It's unthinkable. The moment their minds became one, his soul connected with hers. He remembers that day like it was yesterday. He had just started this project two years ago and suddenly a voice screamed in his head, demanding he allow her inside his workspace. He had spit out his meal. He truly thought he was losing his mind, but Char insisted she was very much real, proving it when she flew into the window he opened for her. She says the bond snapped into place as soon as she flew by him in his workspace. Now, she's as much a part of him as he's a part of her. He hides her here during the day, but she moves freely at night when the rest of his people sleep.

Since I offered to stay and help you brainstorm how to tackle your dilemma, I assume you are compensating me?

He looks up and smiles. Rising from his seat, he walks to his bag and fishes a package out. "But of course, how could you think I'd forget?" Opening the cloth, he lays out on a table pumpkin seeds and her favorite, smoked squirrel.

She flies over to him, her talons scraping the table when she steps toward his offering. She snaps up the squirrel first. *I still don't know how you get it this delectable flavor.*

"A lot of time with smoking wood pellets."

She switches to the pumpkin seeds. *The two of these make a nice combination. I still think you're fattening me up so I can't ever fly out of here.*

"You are one cantankerous soul, Charlotte, dear. Of course, I wouldn't do such a thing."

Being this way only makes me more of an inspiration, Prince.

He huffs. Although he did fashion his machine after a bird, with two wings and a tail. Once he gets to the finishes, he'll paint it the colors Char is so proud of: orange and red.

As it should be.

Duke sighs inwardly, which he knows she hears but chooses to ignore. He paces, keeping his eyes glued to the source of his frustrations. After several passes, he freezes and scratches his jaw with disbelief. "How did I miss it?"

Blaming his overtired mind, he takes his wrench, pries off the gear he's been struggling with and throws it to the side. He dismantles the mechanism and reaches for a smaller gear. He fumbles with it, and with painstaking care, tries to fit it into place. *Of course, the other one wouldn't fit.* It was simply too big. He needs a fresher mind to work on this. However, getting his large fingers to do this job is impossible.

He drops the piece and turns to Char. "I need your help."

She looks at him as if he's got a second head. *Pardon?*

"Unfortunately, I need your help. I remember now that I couldn't fit this wheel into place, so I tried using a bigger size that's clearly not going to work. Just hold this smaller one in place for me while I screw it in."

And how do you propose I do that? She looks at him with such indignation he chuckles.

"Your beak will do."

She rears back in shock. After a moment, she grumbles, *You need an assistant.*

"Well, seeing as it's just you and me, you'll do."

She huffs in displeasure but moves into position, using her beak to hold the piece in place. *Be quick about it.*

He works fast, and with Char's help, secures the piece. "Okay, I'm finished."

Char lets go, and he steps back and looks over his handiwork. Bending forward, he nudges the now appropriately sized wheel to turn, and it sets into motion a procession of movement. He laughs as several gears now glide smoothly together, one after another, all moving in motion. "Yes!"

When I said you'd figure it out, I did not offer my services. Refrain from ever asking for such assistance again. That just cost you more squirrel meat.

Laughing, he turns, his exhaustion forgotten. He crosses the room, picks up his friend and twirls her around his small place, knocking over a broom and scattering a pile of sawdust. She erupts in an indignant squawk.

Put me down at once. Stop manhandling me, Meathead! You're making a mess.

"You only call me that when you're proud of me. Admit it, I'm brilliant." He lets her go, and she spins into the air. Her tail flares in a whoosh of fire as she lands on an iron seat he'd made for her years ago. Flapping her wings to keep her balance, she spreads her feathers out in an undignified whirl of plumage. Even so, she's beautiful.

That will not get you back in my good graces, Prince Blockhead.

"Ah, but my lovely, who will dance with you but me?"

I would not call that *a dance. That was a travesty of steps.*

"Hey, that was my happy dance. Call it ugly, but it was beautiful to me, since it was a celebration."

If you call that beautiful, I have no confidence in your measure of beauty. Now, finish this blasted hunk of wood and metal.

"Don't call it that."

What should I call it then?

"I haven't thought of a name yet. It'll come to me. In a moment of brilliance, I'll think of it."

Uh, huh. I'm off to hunt.

"Thanks, Char. You are my muse, whom I couldn't dream of being without."

With that very unpoetic remark, I leave you to your ... work.

Char doesn't believe he can mimic what she does so brilliantly—fly. He can't wait to prove her wrong.

He smiles fondly as she glides to the hidden window. She nudges the oilskin flap open and flies out into the night.

Duke frowns. She didn't check to make sure no one was around. She always checks. No one is ever up at three in the morning, but they have precautions in place for a reason. If she were discovered, her life would be forfeit.

His impromptu dance must have really flustered her. That and her hunger. She put off finding her meal long enough. His small offering was hardly enough to fill her stomach. And she's not really a touchy-feely kind of pet, claiming she'll burn him one day.

He scoffs. Between his natural elemental abilities and agility, he's never even gotten close to being burned. His greatest elemental strength is fire.

Now that Char's gone, Duke refocuses on his work. He's soon lost in a mess of metal screws, gears, and other pieces he's created to make this majestic machine fly. They're scattered across his detailed plans. The insane idea that he's creating the first flying machine this world has ever known electrifies his blood.

Although, he will never be able to take credit for this one-of-a-kind project, much to his disappointment. He'll have to use an alias and don a disguise to show it off.

But that's the life he's been born into. Concealing his identity is better than nothing. And he despises doing nothing. He puts on a good show, the very picture of sloth and apathy, but inwardly he's seething. This machine is his only way to keep his sanity.

Duke can't stand that his parents want him to live the lazy life of a noble. But it's what they and countless generations before them did, so he supposes he can't fault them. He refuses, however, to embrace it. He'll pretend, but one day this historic achievement will happen. He's made it his life's work.

If only the world could know it was from him.

Chapter Two

The Maid

Elora sits up straight, stretching her aching back. She looks down at the overflowing basket of wet laundry. Scrubbing is finally done.

Taking a moment to catch her breath, she removes the kerchief that holds up her waist-length hair, letting it fall in honey-gold waves around her. A quiet groan escapes her lips.

She peers up at the moon and frowns. It's nearing three in the morning. If she hadn't needed to check on her mother before her washing duties, Elora would be sleeping. Her mother had an especially hard night and couldn't keep anything down. Knowing the importance of hydration, Elora encouraged her mother to keep down a couple sips of water just over an hour ago.

Her mother had succumbed to the wasting illness that ravaged the land a year ago. But while most others recovered after receiving vampire venom, she and her father couldn't afford it.

If it became known her mother is still sick, they would be cast out of the fae kingdom, like many others who couldn't afford the costly medicine. The highly contagious disease was feared. But Elora had come up with a protection system where her father and herself could escape its clutches by wearing masks and gloves and constantly washing their hands with soapwort.

Casting her eyes up at the vast expanse of the sky, she admires the sparkling stars blinking down at her. Her heart is so sore, she would love to be a star and happily watch the lives happening below her. Dreaming is easy; it's living that's hard.

Picking up a wet sheet, she clips it onto the clothesline that stretches along the back of the garden. She's working on the very edge of the palace property, and as she continues, she scans row upon row of succulent vegetables in the moonlight. They're tended by her father as one of the royal gardeners. Just looking at them makes her stomach clench painfully. She had forgone her dinner to help her mother get settled, and then she had to start the laundry.

Reaching for one of the Prince Heir's shirts, she pins it to the clothesline. She's mildly intrigued to be working with one of his shirts and not his younger brother's attire. There's something about the Prince Heir that makes you look twice, an allure his younger brother doesn't share. Despite keeping her eyes down, she couldn't help but notice the elder prince. However, she doesn't want any attention; attention only means she'll be required to do yet another task for the royal family.

She reflects on the prince's looks. He's not classically handsome, but his face is interesting. It's one that when he looks your way, you can't help straightening your spine in his intense perusal. His nose is slightly too large and his lips a touch thin, but despite his faults, she's always found him handsome. She doesn't love, however, his lazing away every day. Elora punches down revulsion for his lifestyle. It's not her business what he does with his time. She can only shake her head at the many times she's seen him lying around doing *nothing*.

She can't imagine such a life.

Elora may not enjoy her work, but she does like being busy. Keeping her hands full and her mind engaged, especially with her mother sick, has been a blessing. She bites her lip in thought. She's been brainstorming ways to make enough coin to pay for the venom her mother so desperately needs. Her mother will succumb soon if something isn't done. Could Elora start baking on the side? But between her caring for her mother and her duties at the palace, she doesn't have much time.

She has to think of something.

Movement in the corner of her eye makes her whip her head toward the right. A large red and orange bird flies past her into the night.

There's no way that's a phoenix.

Phoenixes are highly feared and outlawed. One spark could incinerate the entire town of treehouses. Her pulse races. She's always wanted to see one of these elusive birds since she was a little girl. There's something so magical about a bird that can sport flames all over its body. The mere thought she can glimpse one now has her leaving her chore. She squints and rushes to follow. Was it even a phoenix? She's only ever seen pictures in a book. Since they're hunted, they avoid any fae area.

Running, she steps carefully to avoid crunching any branches or leaves. She quickly makes her way toward where she last saw the reclusive bird. She catches a glimpse of a red tail and jogs toward it. Once she reaches the area she last saw it, Elora stops and looks all around. Listening, she thinks she hears a flap of wings up ahead. Putting on a burst of speed, she runs in that direction, craning her head everywhere to spot it. By now, she's run to the very edge of the town. She hopes this journey out here is not in vain. No one lives out here. There's only abandoned underground bunkers. *Maybe I scared it off?* Thinking if she hides, it might come out again, she slips behind a fir tree. After a few moments, she peers around the trunk.

Disappointment drops her shoulders when she doesn't see the bird. But then she spies something just as unusual. A light in one of the old underground bunkers.

But that can't be.

The higher you live in a treehouse, the more royal your blood. The lower you live, the least of the social caste you are. She lives in one of the lowest homes in the town, but to choose to live underground is unthinkable. No sane person would dare claim such a place. Did the phoenix fly into it and light something within on fire? If so, she needs to sound an alarm. It's either that or it's an insane fae, the only kind that would live in such a dirty space. She walks toward it.

What will I find?

With trepidatious steps, she continues.

Chapter Three

The Prince

A branch cracks outside. Duke's head whips up. Exhaustion forgotten, he drops his tools and shoots to his feet. In hurried, silent steps, he creeps to the door. He pauses to listen.

Char would never make a sound like that, he's sure of it.

Slender fingers move the oilskin covering the window that's right by the door. A feminine gasp follows when the interloper gets an eyeful of his work.

His heart pounds in his chest. It's a feminine hand, but even so, he doesn't have an option; he must question this intruder. *How did she find this place? No one is out at this time of night.*

He grabs her hand, pulling her arm through the window. A short scream fills the air, and when her head appears, he clamps his other hand over her mouth.

Her muffled protests and flashing eyes tell him she's furious at his manhandling. His royal manners come through immediately, and he says. "I'm sorry, my lad ... y." He's yanked enough of her inside that he sees her black and white maid uniform. "Er...just stop screaming, and I will let you go. But you must promise not to run away when I do."

Jerky head movements promise she'll stay, so he lets her go.

She shimmies back outside and when he looks out the window, he sees her racing away. "Blast it!" He throws open the door, and he's outside in a blink. She got a head start, but he puts on a burst of speed and catches up to her. He grabs her by the waist. Swinging her around, he pulls her back to his chest and clamps a hand over her mouth again, cutting off another ear-splitting shriek.

She struggles in his arms, but she's no match for his strength. Her warming hands tell him she's trying to use the element of fire to make him drop her, but his own much stronger gifting overpowers her smaller one. Dragging her to the hidden doorway of his formerly private space, he whispers in her ear, "I'm not going to hurt you. I just need to talk to you."

At his words, she stiffens. She peers over her shoulder, and when she gets a look at his face, her eyes widen in surprise.

Now that she knows who he is, he must make sure she agrees to remain quiet about his not-so-princely nighttime activities. She relaxes in his arms as he pulls her back to the bunker.

He turns his head to hide his smile. He has this effect on most fae women. But then he groans in frustration. *Why did she have to find his secret workspace?*

Not trusting her to come quietly, he kicks apart old vines that have grown on the door. With his hand still on the maid's mouth, he lets go of her trim waist and uses his free hand to twist the handle.

He runs through what reward he could give her to assure her silence and the preservation of his secret. He could never find another location like this. He must find a way to convince her.

Pulling her through the door, he kicks it shut and eases his hand away from her mouth. She immediately spins around, fire flashing in her eyes. Shock jolts through him at the sight. He recognizes her as one of the palace maids with her white apron and black dress, but never has he seen her beauty showcased in fury like this.

Her hair fans out, falling around her shoulders like a waterfall, a wavy, glorious sight. Usually, she keeps her hair hidden behind fabric. He can't help but admire the color; his region is known for darker locks, but the gold in hers is hypnotizing. And her eyes. They match her hair, honey gold and burning with frenzied desperation. She tucks her hair behind her elegant, pointed ears and pins him with a stare.

Get your head on straight, Prince, this one is not for you.

Distance doesn't matter to his mind-melded friend. She can see everything through his mind. So even though he doesn't see her, she hears his thoughts, and he shoves down her reprimand.

He growls in response. The maid's eyes widen, and she backs up toward the door.

He holds up his hands. "I'm not upset with you."

She looks around warily. "Who might you be upset with then? I'm the only one here. Unless you can see ghosts."

He can't help it. He quirks a grin at the thought of Char as a spirit of the night.

As if I would be such a thing. I'll show her a far more glorious sight than that.

"Don't you dare." He presses his lips shut, not meaning to speak out loud. Now this woman thinks he's berating her. Frustrated, he runs his hands through his hair.

It's bad enough someone found his lair. He's desperate enough to find a way to ensure her silence. Because the secret of Char could not get out.

Stay hidden, Char.

Chapter Four

The Maid

"Who do you think you are, talking to and manhandling me like that?"

Surprise replaces the look of irritation on the prince's face.

Elora studies him, and it takes all her concentration to remain upright. She locks her weak knees. His dark hair hangs loose around his shoulders, giving him a rakish air. His shirt hangs untucked from his dark pants, but he's left the front open enough she can see a span of muscles the shirt hides. He's always been good looking to her. But up close, he makes her head spin. She starts taking tiny steps toward the door. His bright green eyes track her small movements knowingly.

Half of his mouth quirks up in a smile. "I think we both know who I am." He straightens to his full height. The way he holds himself intrigues her despite her not wanting to be intrigued. It's like he knows his value, his worth, but isn't shoving it at her. He quietly assumes she knows.

She stops her half steps toward the door.

Waving her hands around, she splutters, "Well, just because you're the prince doesn't give you the right to put your hands all over me..."

"Whoa, stop right there." He holds out his palms. "I did not put my hands all over you." His grin disappears.

Elora glares up at him. *Why does he have to be so blasted tall?* "What do you think your hand on my mouth and around my waist was called?"

He takes a step back, surprise again taking over his expression. "Usually, a fae woman wouldn't complain about that."

Irritation flashes through her. "Oh, and I'm to enjoy you muzzling me then, forcing me down into this filthy hole?" She's insane to talk to the prince like this, but she can't seem to stop her mouth.

Regret fills his eyes. "I do apologize for that. But I had to silence your screams."

"Well, I could have gone my whole life without this experience. Despite how many fae women might enjoy it."

He smiles like he knows something she doesn't. "Again, you have my deepest apologies. Although as intriguing as this conversation has been, we need to talk."

"About what? Where are we?" She turns around, and her words are lost when she looks around the space. From the window, she'd glimpsed a sliver of an amazing craft, but to see it in all its glory takes her breath away.

It's quite large, barely fitting onto a sizeable worktable. It's a contraption she's never seen before that resembles a small canoe with long wooden pieces coming out of its sides, like bird wings and an open maw of interlocking metal pieces on one end with two more smaller wood pieces affixed to the front.

"We need to talk about that," he says, his expression sobering. He points at the contraption. "And we are in my lair."

She laughs. She can't help it. "A *lair*? Is this what you call this dirty space?"

He frowns and looks around, his lips pressed together. "It's not dirty. I'll have you know I keep it quite clean."

"Oh, really? Explain the dirt floors then." Elora points to the ground.

The prince rubs his neck. "I didn't want to waste time building a wooden floor. I am rather busy."

Elora nods, still studying whatever that is on the worktable. "I can see that. Is that a canoe? Why on earth would you need a boat in the middle of the forest?" She studies it, walking to the table and around it, examining it from all angles.

He clenches his jaw. "No, it's not a canoe. And why wouldn't I want a watercraft, anyway? The coast is only half a league away."

She taps her finger on her lips. "I guess. Well?"

"*That* is a secret. And it must stay that way."

"So that's why you're hidden down in this dirty place. You chose somewhere no one would ever stumble upon this ... thing."

"Not dirty," the Prince mumbles.

An idea takes root in her mind, and once it enters, she can't unthink it. *It's clear he's hiding this thing. He would do anything, pay anything, to keep this quiet. This would solve all her problems. She must try.* Her whole body rejects this insane plan, because she's not the kind of person to do this, but there's no other way.

"You need to keep this a secret?" she asks slowly, flicking a glance at him, then away just as quickly.

A knowing expression takes over his face, and he crosses his arms. "Yes," he says in a low voice. "How much would it cost for your silence?"

She half turns, her mind abhorring such a terrible choice. An awful guilt nearly crushes her. *But no, there is no other way. She has to do this. She finally has a chance to save her mother.* Biting her lip, she then says in a rush, "I would say, five thousand pounds would do it."

His eyebrows hike, and his eyes flash in outrage. "You're robbing me blind with that sum!"

"No, I'm not robbing, exactly," Elora hedges, fingering her sleeve.

"Extorting," he huffs and looks away, his jaw working. He turns back at her. "You could quit serving in the palace with that kind of coin."

She bristles. "I'm not trying to leave my position."

"Then what would you do with it?"

She spins toward him, her black and white skirts swirling. "That is *none* of your business." No one can find out about her mother. No matter what. Especially him. He'd force her mother to leave their land in a minute if he knew the truth.

The prince leans back on his heels. "I think it's very much my business. It's my money after all."

"Well, you're not going to get a reason." Elora stands firm, her body vibrating with protective anger. Her mother is not healthy enough to travel. Only the venom can help her now.

"If you need that much money, why don't you sell your blood?" He cocks his eyebrow.

Fae blood is hard to get in other lands and highly valued. Fae hardly ever leave Nebraria. Their blood adds substantially more power to the creature who pairs it with goblin white crystals. They finally had to guard their borders against opportunists trying to come in and kidnap fae to extract their blood.

She shakes her head. "I can't afford the time it would it take to recover from giving it. I need my job at the palace too much." Plus, any moment she has to spare, goes to the care of her mother. Her father, too, can't take time off. It takes the two of them to take care of her ailing mother.

The prince studies her for a moment and then puts his hands on his hips. He shakes his head, looking down. "I can't get my hands on that kind of money right away. But maybe..."

Hope soars through her. If he can gather even a portion, she can afford a small vial of the venom, which would save her mother's life and extend it by *weeks*. "How much *can* you acquire?"

An annoyed look crosses his face. "A third of the amount you're blackmailing me for."

She rounds on him. "You must have known you'd have to pay for my silence."

"Not with that kind of money I didn't." His look turned contemplative. "If you're not trying to escape your lifestyle, I can only imagine why you'd need that amount. Do you owe someone money?"

"Hardly," slips out of Elora's mouth before she can stop it. It would be better if he thought she owed someone that kind of sum. Anything to keep his curiosity away from her sick mother and vampire venom.

"Hmm," is all he says.

She turns toward the door with one last lingering look at the interesting wooden craft. She would love to study it, but she forces herself to open the door. Forgetting a very major part of this agreement, she turns around and sticks her hand out. "Do we have a bargain?"

His entire body stiffens. "You want a binding agreement?"

She scoffs. "Of course. I'm not stupid."

"My word isn't enough?"

Thinking of his lazy lifestyle, she snorts. "No." But then she thinks of his secret she's agreeing to keep. He's hiding more of who he is and what he's interested in than anyone knows. There would be plenty who would pay to have this kind of knowledge. However, she would not stoop to such measures. This is bad enough.

With a resigned air, he sticks his hand out. As soon as he grasps her hand, she says the words that will bind them together until he pays all the money. "In keeping with all honesty, the Prince Heir of the Fae lands, Duke Williams, agrees to pay five thousand pounds to Elora Wincham for her silence on his ... hidden proclivities." She fuels her words with the power of her fae blood.

She knows that the last part is vague, but he will have her silence about what she's learned tonight. Knowing him to be somewhat honorable, she must trust that this binding will not require her to hide a murder or anything nefarious.

They shake, and a bright, golden cord snakes around their hands and wrists, burning into the skin, leaving a heat that's unbearable at first but cools quickly. The permanence of what she just did shakes her. The light fades slowly, and she says with trembling lips, "Please don't become a horrible criminal and expect me to hide your deeds."

He smirks. "I wouldn't dream of it."

Elora looks into his eyes for a long moment and realizes she hasn't yet released his huge hand. She drops it immediately. "Yes, well, I'll have to take your word on that."

"Oh, my dear, I think you have much more than a promise." He looks meaningfully down at her hand, where a lingering sparkle rests on her skin. That will fade by the morning, but he's right.

What has she gotten herself into?

Chapter Five

The Prince

After Elora leaves, Duke's body sags. He looks down at the sparkles on his hand and arm. The remnant of the bargain he just struck forces him to sigh deeply.

Then he cracks a grim smile. Elora forgot one very important caveat of that bargain. She didn't say when he would be required to deliver the money. He could take her whole lifetime to pay her. However, allowing her to hold the power of that bargain over his head is not acceptable, especially when she carries his secret. There are ways she could reveal his project without actually telling anyone about it.

She also seems to desperately need the money. He wouldn't want her in any kind of danger. Just thinking of her in that position makes him shift uncomfortably.

Char flies back into the room and from her perch on one of her many seats, glares at his arm. *You've gotten yourself into quite a pickle, Prince.*

"I know." Then, he eyes her with annoyance. "And what did you mean by wanting to meet her? Have you lost your mind?"

If a phoenix could shrug, she does. *She would just have to keep me a secret, too. Besides, I didn't lure her here for nothing.*

Duke's head snaps up. "What?"

Char turns her head. *Let's just say I have a feeling about her.*

Duke runs a hand through his hair. "Are you telling me, Elora found my secret space because of *you*?"

What part of lure did you not understand?

"Char, that's too much of a gamble! You are outlawed here. She could turn you in. I can't risk that. And now my secret project is no longer a secret. Blast it! I had to submit to a bargain because of you!"

I should not be a secret, dear Prince and neither should your work. Besides, our connection alone should convince others of my worth.

Her tone is surprisingly gentle. Char is only kind when she wants something. He wonders where she's going with that statement.

It's time you told someone about me.

"Tell *her*?" he whisper shouts, pointing at the door. "Someone I'm paying off to keep this place secret?"

She seems intelligent enough to keep one more secret. It would behoove you to trust someone.

"A woman, no less?"

Her eyes glitter. *I've always said you need a princess. Someone with mettle who can take you down a peg or two. She seems to fit that description.*

"Char, she's *blackmailing* me. Not a good start for a relationship. Besides, my people would revolt if I chose a servant as my wife."

So, convince them you are not who you claim to be. Convince them you are more than qualified to choose the right queen.

"In *her*?" he shakes his head hard. "I'm too tired for this conversation. I'm going to bed."

Don't forget to scrounge up those five thousand pounds. And think about what I said.

At those words, she flies to the window, this time verifying a clear exit. When she seems satisfied no more surprise guests will see her, she flies out into the darkness.

Rubbing his face, feeling more weary than ever before, Duke thinks over his situation. It's not the money he's concerned with; it's Elora's actual silence. He can't help but smile at her pluck. She's been quite the distraction this night. *What did he just get himself into?* Binding himself to someone is not ideal. But he didn't have much of a choice. If he, for some reason, does not pay the money, his hand will be crippled, burned wherever the golden threads of the binding touched. Unthinkable, considering it would be very difficult to complete his flying machine with one hand. Even without the distinction of saying when he needs to deliver, he will pay. That's a risk he's not willing to take.

The maid literally has his life's work in her small hands.

Not the maid. Elora. What a pretty name. He tries not to think of how she looked while flashing her bright molten eyes at him. And with her hair cascading all around her, she looked...glorious. He wondered whether she had meant to wear it loose like that. She looked wild and free, untamed.

Fae women tended to be more controlled and prim in attitude and appearance. They kept their hair pinned back or up, so it was a rare treat seeing Elora's tresses unbound. Her demand, however, also surprised him. Five thousand pounds is an enormous amount.

As he turns down the oil lamp, he's relieved Elora didn't see Char. She is one secret he will have to guard more carefully. Until Elora is paid, Char will have to stay away. He sighs. Char won't like that. She already revealed herself once tonight.

He scans the room to be sure he's extinguished all the lamps. His bleary eyes had missed one before, and he never heard the end of it from Char after she had to come in and put one out. Which, according to her, was difficult, since she has claws instead of nimble fingers like his.

With one more loving look at his craft, he peers through the window to be sure the coast is clear. When he's sure it is, he heads to the tree palace with tired steps. Its size alone marks it as royal, but its height, too, gives it that distinction. It's a constant source of pride to his parents. All the homes are built into enormous redwood trees, the largest in Lurin. One redwood tree is the size of ten full-grown fir trees. And the palace is built into the largest redwood in the forest. The town grew around the palatial structure.

Elora is long gone, but he probably wouldn't have seen her anyway with the servants' staircase being on the opposite side of the massive trunk. He wonders what she was doing up at this hour of the night. In his stunned state, he hadn't thought to ask.

Duke had noticed her before in the palace rooms. Any fae man could appreciate her unique beauty.

Forcing thoughts of her perfect lips away as he starts the long climb up the palace stairs, he tries to consider her appearance objectively. He can't, however. Her chin, like her mouth, balances beautifully to her cheekbones that aren't high like the typical fae woman; her face is more oval, instead of narrow. But it's her eyes that are truly mesmerizing. The color of pure honey, they sparkled in a way that didn't stop him from appreciating the amber gems, even when she narrowed them at him. He's suddenly curious to see what they look like when she's laughing or happy. She seemed pleased when he accepted her bargain. But it wasn't enough.

How things have changed tonight, he thinks as he walks down the royal hallway. The idea that even one person besides Char knows of his true nature makes him smile. He enters his rooms and readies for bed as most are preparing to awaken, wondering for the first time what tomorrow will bring.

Chapter Six

The Prince

Duke wakes up in an exceptionally good mood. One he can't get his foggy brain to wrap around, considering what happened last night. When the enormity of the situation passes through his mind, he sits up with a lurch, holding his head in his hands. He owes the maid five thousand pounds, a third of which he's sure she will come to collect tonight.

"My Prince? Is all well?" Grant, his personal manservant, looks at him with no small amount of concern while holding Duke's clothing for the day.

Duke masks his face with the usual one of utter boredom. "Just a bad dream, Grant. Do not be concerned."

If only it were a dream. He looks down at his hand and arm, where the binding waits for him to fulfill. He can almost see the faint glimmer it left behind. Hiding his arm under the covers, he hopes Grant won't notice. As loyal as Grant is to him, Duke doesn't want to test it with the knowledge of a bargain.

He looks out the window, noting it's well into the afternoon. Keeping his face still, he wonders if Elora had a chance to rest last night, or rather, this morning, before rising again to fulfill her duties. He can't help his concern; she can't afford to live the worthless life he lives. Not worthless, he reminds himself. He's got a purpose, even if it's hidden.

And the fact that *someone* besides Char knows about it lifts his spirits.

Am I so unimportant that my silence doesn't count? Char's voice jars his thoughts.

Eyeing Grant, who busied himself again with laying out the princely clothes, he makes sure to think, 'No, my dear Char, you are a prize any fae would be lucky to have in his corner. But please cease this talk of revealing yourself to anyone but me.'

You should be at your full potential. Not laze your days away.

'We are in full agreement, but you know I can't change history,' he mulls silently.

You certainly can.

He sighs inwardly. 'Please Charlotte. Let me think for a moment.'

He notices Grant's skeptical glances and wonders what his face must have revealed of that conversation.

Extending his leg, Duke makes a show of getting up slowly, yawning widely. "What's on the schedule for today, Grant?"

"My Prince, the queen has scheduled you to have tea with Ladies Mary and Elizabeth Strafford in one hour."

Duke groans and then ponders for a moment. His mother is as tenacious as Char at getting him married. There's a statement in that selection. His mother must want something from the Strafford family.

What could it be?

As droll as palace life can be, one thing it doesn't lack is politics. There are always social maneuvering and plots happening all over the place. It's one reason why his parents want him at every gathering the palace has. He's expected to forge relationships with the nobles so he can have their support when he's king.

He keeps abreast of all agendas and has confidants in place to provide him with necessary information. One of those is his manservant. "Are the Straffords in any way associated with the Expansion Act?"

Grant hums as he shakes out the non-existent wrinkles in Duke's pants. "Most assuredly, my Prince. They are at the forefront of wanting to build the next city."

Another fae city does not worry Duke, but it would concern his mother, who wants all noble life to center around the palace. Another city would take precious courtiers away from her watchful eyes.

"They are unsatisfied with their place in the treehouse?"

Grant harrumphs. "It would appear so. The center of the tree is far too low for the likes of them. They wish to elevate themselves, my Prince." He sniffs as if it's preposterous for any fae to want more of life than what they are given. "If the act passes, they will have top-tier access."

Duke walks over to the dutifully prepared clothes and plucks his shirt, throwing it on casually. "So, these sisters are not interested in my hand?"

Grant chokes, then clears his throat, apologizing. "My Prince, these two sisters would do just about anything to be queen. Another fae city is not their desire, only their father's."

Duke squashes down frustration. What he would give to be appreciated for his mind and not his title.

Anything is the short answer to that. And I know just the person to do it.

He winces at Char's words. He tries to shut down his thoughts, so they don't blare out into the expanse to his dear pet phoenix. Still, he can't help but wonder if she's right.

Of course I am.

He presses his lips together and finishes dressing, not understanding what Char sees in that minx who would rob him blind for her silence.

He sits down in a chair in his water closet, leaning back so Grant can begin his daily shave. While Grant readies his razor, Duke asks in an off-hand way, "Grant, I'm in need of seventeen hundred pounds. Have it ready for me by this evening."

"Milord?" Grant gives him a befuddled look.

Duke smiles in a cavalier way. "Is that a problem?"

"No, of course not. But your mother..."

"Ah yes, my mother will want to know what the funds are for."

"Yes, my Prince," Grant says after hesitating. "She will. Please excuse my attention on this." His face flushes in embarrassment at being caught between him and his indomitable mother.

"Just tell her it's for my gaming amusement."

"Yes, milord."

Grant finishes shaving Duke in his normal, timely manner. Duke has just enough time to make his way to the parlor. He tries to ignore his empty stomach and his guilt over his obvious lie. As far as the first, if he had woken up an hour earlier, he would have satisfied his enormous appetite with a large brunch. As for the latter, Grant knows the allowances given to both princes. This far extends his allotted amount for the month. But there's no denying a prince what he wants. Duke will just have to come up with a convincing story for his dear mother.

He hides a cringe. That he will need a total of five thousand pounds has not escaped him. He'll figure something out. Burning flares in his wrist, reminding him it's not the whole amount due.

As he opens the door to the drawing room, he sees the two sisters sitting primly next to a tray of small sandwiches. He should have eaten something before this infernal tea. Now he will be limited to those small excuses for sandwiches, even tinier cakes, and rich tea. At least he can look forward to giving his system a jolt of energy with the tea he favors.

Half bemused, he notes that the sisters' dark hair has been tucked up into elaborate hairstyles befitting their status. Before

Elora last night, he'd never considered seeing a fae woman with her hair down, but Elora quickly changed his mind. However, glancing at these two women, he finds no desire to see their hair loose.

Rousing himself out of his thoughts, he ambles toward them, saying, "Lady Mary, Lady Elizabeth, how lovely you two look this morning, er, afternoon."

They titter behind their hands at his mistake and smile primly. Elora's face flashes through his mind again, and he wonders for the second time what her smile looks like.

As if he conjured her, a maid appears in the corner of his eye, and he turns his head a fraction to see if it's her. Disappointment follows when it's not Elora, but another whose name escapes him. The maid doesn't let his attention go before she smiles demurely. Frowning, he gives his attention to the two sisters, immediately launching into gossip he knows the sisters will love.

He's in the middle of describing the disastrous act of a broken teapot when someone catches his attention behind the sisters' heads. A rush fills his veins when Elora brings in a tray with a tea refill. She avoids his eyes, and his mind stalls.

"My Prince, you were saying..." Lady Mary says, with an eager glint in her eyes.

"Uh, yes." He scrambles to finish his story as Elora approaches. He watches her as she expertly replaces the empty teapot with a full one, not spilling a drop. "The maid, er, tipped the pot too hard and the whole thing went crashing onto the floor."

Elora fumbles with the empty pot but recovers quickly, and with firm hands fills the empty tray with the used plates and cups. She turns to leave.

Not wanting her to go just yet, he says, "Elora, is it? Would the kitchens have any pastries on hand, by any chance?"

He doesn't miss Lady Mary's frown at him, asking Elora a direct question and his knowledge of her name.

Elora keeps her eyes down, but her blush is telling enough. "Uh, yes, Milord, I believe so."

"Please bring them to me, I mean, us."

Finally, her eyes latch onto his, and after hesitating, she says, "I have just the thing."

It's like she's trying to communicate something to him, but he can't imagine what it is. He sits back, waves her away, like he's the indifferent prince he pretends to be, and resumes his attention on the two sisters.

Lady Elizabeth gives Elora a small smile, looking at her like she's a puzzle. Lady Mary, however, doesn't hide her anger, flattening her lips. "Really, my Prince," she objects, "is it necessary to ask her to bring something else? Don't we have plenty?" She looks over the tray of cakes and sandwiches.

"No," he drawls. "These are not to my taste. I desire something else."

That much is true. It's clear to him in that moment that he would much rather spend time with the enigmatic maid than these two noble ladies. He notes that Lady Elizabeth is much more tolerable than her sister, but still, he wishes to coax a smile from Elora.

He bought himself some time with the fair maid, in more ways than in the pastries because of their bargain, but it surprises him that he doesn't mind. Not when she's coming back.

He continues the predictable conversation with the sisters, drowning in boredom. When Elora returns, he forces himself not to straighten from his relaxed posture. Lady Mary visibly stiffens as Elora sets a tray down. Lady Elizabeth just looks on with curiosity.

His stomach grumbles. Elora has brought the most delectable apple tarts. They're his favorite. Did she know?

He looks up at her with carefully disguised surprise, giving her a crooked smile. "These will do. My thanks."

A pretty blush covers both cheeks as she dishes up one of the tarts and hands him the plate, looking at him almost shyly.

She bites her lip. "I made these just ... last night. I hope you enjoy them."

"That is not your place, Maid," Lady Mary barks.

He almost drops the plate in surprise.

Lady Mary yanks the plate from his hand and glares at Elora. "We will serve the Prince."

This time, Elora's blush is of sure embarrassment. "I ... I apologize, Milady. I'll leave you to your tea."

"Honestly, the *nerve*," Lady Mary says as Elora flees from the room, glaring at her the whole time.

"Mary," Lady Elizabeth hisses, embarrassment over her sister's ugly behavior becoming obvious.

Duke forces himself not to follow Elora's escape with his eyes. "I'm sure she meant no harm, Lady Mary." He can only hope Elora hears his admonition before she leaves the room.

"She should know better. If she were in my home, I would have her fired immediately," Lady Mary grouses, brushing sugar off the rim of his plate before she hands it to him.

Lady Elizabeth's lips thin in displeasure, and Duke finds himself asking, "And you, Lady Elizabeth, would such an infraction rate a dismissal with you as well?"

She flashes him an unguarded look, seeming almost wounded. "No," she says quietly before she looks down again. "It would not, my Prince."

Lady Mary huffs but stays silent.

Duke sits back and thinks about the interaction. Lady Elizabeth shows rare compassion among the nobility, a trait he greatly admires.

Then his thoughts drift to when Elora could have made such a dish, since they were both up until almost four in the morning. Did she prepare his favorite pastry this morning before she went to bed? Did she know it is his favorite pastry?

Without waiting to think more on it, he sinks his teeth into the softest, flakiest crust. They're just the way he likes. Crisp on the edges and soft in the center. He groans in enjoyment, and his eyes pop open at the noise.

Both sisters watch him avidly, and he hides his embarrassment with a wipe of his napkin. "These are my favorite and perfectly made."

He'll be sure Elora knows it when he sees her tonight.

Chapter Seven

The Maid

Elora leaves the door open a fraction. She knows it's punishing her to see if the prince likes her baking, but she can't help herself. When she hears his subsequent groan of delight, it makes her heart soar. As much as she appreciated his admonishment of Lady Mary's words, it's this reaction that makes her chest tight with excitement.

Smiling widely, she ducks her head when Grant, the prince's manservant, walks up to the door, frowning deeply at her.

"Elora, what are you doing standing there?" he asks, looking around. He's holding a small tray with an envelope on it.

Biting her lip, she thinks fast for an answer, trying to look innocent. "Uh, well, I was making sure they didn't need my services any longer, sir."

His eyebrows furrow. "By standing next to an open door?"

Genuine distress purses her lips. "Well, it seems my presence offends Lady Mary, sir. But I wanted to be close by if the prince needs me for anything else."

Grant's eyes flick to the scene in the cracked-open doorway. "Hmm, I see. Yes, well, I will find you if the prince is in need. Thank you, Elora. Return to your duties."

"Yes, sir," she rushes to say and then flees down the hallway toward the servants' staircase to escape to the kitchens. Embarrassment rushes through her that Grant caught her snooping, but she can't find it in herself to care. Knowing the prince loved her tart made all her efforts in the early morning worth his reaction. She had been so thankful for their bargain that she had stayed up to bake them before she finally went to bed. She had wanted to assuage her guilt of blackmailing the prince, so she had made his favorite pastry. She only knew it was his favorite because it's hers too and she had gotten her hand smacked by the head baker when she had tried to take one.

As she hurries down the staircase, her smile widens at his unguarded enjoyment of her creation. He had said it was perfect. Thoughts swirl about what to make him next. Now that she knows he appreciates her baking, it makes her want to double her efforts. She'll switch shifts with Candy again so she can stay up late tonight.

Knowing she'll see the prince again so soon leaves her feeling a heady rush of excitement. Then the thought that he'll have money for her to pay for her mother's medicine crashes her back to earth.

What kind of person was she to blackmail the prince?

A desperate one.

Hardening her heart against the guilt crushing her, she continues down the staircase, reaching the kitchens at the bottom level easily enough.

Candy spies her and rounds on her, whispering, "Where did you find those apple tarts? You disappeared and then reappeared with them almost as if by magic! They didn't make them this morning." She folds her arms across her chest and taps her foot.

Edging around her dear friend, she hedges, "I found them, that's all. They must have been made yesterday." Wincing at her lies, she tries to leave, but Candy yanks her back. "What are you hiding, my dearest friend?"

Candy's capacity to ferret out any kind of lies rears its ugly head. Applying for mercy from her relentless friend, she asks, "Can you just drop it, please? I can't explain."

Candy hesitates and then asks softly, "Were you baking again because of your mother?"

Elora looks down. Candy knows baking is Elora's one reprieve from the world and her mother's illness. She's also the one fae who knows of her mother's true condition. She nods, hoping that this will satisfy her friend.

"Well, in that case, I guess it's fine. You know if you baked for Paula, she'd throw the palace pastry chef out on his ear and install you instantly."

Paula, the master chef of the royal kitchens, is notoriously difficult to impress, and Elora doubts Candy's confidence. Besides, the proof that the prince loves her baking fills any need to impress anyone.

Elora shakes her head. "I'm fine with my lot in life, Candy."

A voice makes her jump. "Standing around again, Elora? And you, Candy? What is your reason for this?" Grant peers his nose down at them.

"I ... I ... I'm sorry, sir. It won't happen again," Elora stammers. "I just had something to discuss with Candy. We'll return to our duties right away."

He sniffs. "See that you do. Laziness is for the royals. Not for you two."

A hot blush covers Elora's face, the prince's secret bursting in her. Almost as in warning, her wrist flares hot. She rubs it gently.

Candy yanks Elora's arm and drags her to the laundry room. When they're safe behind the thick wooden door, she hisses, "I swear, something has gotten into you. What was that look on your face just now?"

Elora rubs her wrist as it flares again, saying, "Nothing! I just started thinking about all the work I have to do."

Candy studies Elora and then walks straight toward the huge bins where an endless supply of dirty laundry sits waiting to be scrubbed. Elora follows meekly. She'd love to confide in her friend about everything that happened overnight, but she never can. Not if she wants full use of her hand and arm. Her bargain with the prince has no time limit on either side, so she is obligated to hide his true activities for the rest of her life. She'll carry his secret to her grave.

She really should have thought that through more carefully. Despair fills her that the prince might not give her the coin she so desperately needs in a timely manner. Technically, he isn't bound to that detail. *Why hadn't she put a time limit on that bargain?*

"Elora!" Candy shoves her, knocking her from her reveries.

"What?" Elora looks blankly at her.

"I said, what if the King and Queen want the prince to meet other princesses? Like a siren or a werewolf?"

Elora frowns, for some reason her stomach twists at the thought. "Has that ever been done before? I mean, we're all at peace with each other. It would only make sense if we were at war and desperate for a way to unite our kingdoms."

Candy shrugs and grins at her friend. "I wouldn't mind meeting a brawny werewolf who comes to visit our court. Can you imagine?"

She really couldn't. Being isolated had never felt so restricting. *What would it be like to travel? Would she ever know?*

Candy bumps her shoulder. "Why the sad face?"

The reality of her station has never hit her so hard before. She's always been at peace with her situation. How did one night talking to the fae prince change her feelings about her suddenly dismal future?

She sighs. "Oh, it's nothing. I'd like to see some of Lurin, that's all."

Candy drops the sheet she was scrubbing. "Why don't you?"

Elora looks at her sadly. "You know I could never leave my mother."

"Oh. Of course. I'm sorry, Elora." She puts her wet hand on Elora's shoulder. "Maybe someday?"

"Yes," Elora sighs. "One day."

That day might only ever happen in her dreams, but she promises herself if she can find a way in her lifetime to do more than cook and clean, she'll do it.

Until then, she'll make the best of her life.

Even if she has to blackmail a prince to do it.

Chapter Eight

The Prince

Duke moderates his steps after bowing and leaving the Strafford sisters, wanting to run down the hall, but forcing himself to exercise restraint. He had never been so bored in his life. Well, he's had some terrible conversations in his time at court, but today's mundanity took the cake.

If he had to discuss one more fashion accessory, he might have exploded. Instead, all he could do was paint a smile on his face and suffer through it.

"What has you so glum-faced?" Harry, his brother, slaps Duke's shoulder.

Masking his emotions and his surprise at failing to notice his brother, he stops walking. "Oh, it's nothing."

Harry laughs. "If I were a betting man, which I am, I would say you're depressed considering the possibility of marriage to one of those sisters." He points behind Duke's shoulder.

Duke looks at his younger brother with new respect. "Well, place your bets and prepare to win."

"Were they that bad, brother? They are attractive enough, I'd say. I saw them leaving just now."

Duke continues down the hallway to his rooms. He sighs. "They are what's to be expected of well brought up young ladies." He pauses. "They're just so *predictable.*" His thoughts swing to Elora, and he smiles. He's positive she's well brought up, too, but her passionate nature contradicts everything he's known of fae women.

"Yes, I see what you mean." Then he glances at Duke. "Hey, what's that smile now? Oh, ho, are you thinking of another fair maiden?"

Duke wipes his smile off his face. "No, of course not."

Harry stops him from walking, holding his shoulders. "I wasn't born yesterday, brother of mine. I know interest when I see it."

Duke shrugs Harry's hands off and pushes past him. "Well, you're wrong. I'm not interested in anyone. And please do not spill your suspicions to our mother. That's the last thing I need."

Harry keeps up with Duke's long stride. "I'll keep my mouth shut only if you admit there is a woman in your thoughts."

Duke blows out a frustrated breath. What is it with people learning his secrets? Was he so transparent?

Harry stops and turns in the other direction. "I mean it. I'll go straight to Mother. Right now."

Lurching to a stop, Duke's at his brother's side in one stride. "Do. Not. Do that."

Harry chuckles. "Then, spill, brother. Admit it. That's all I demand."

Not willing to call his brother's bluff, he grits out. "Fine. Someone did occupy my thoughts. *Momentarily.*"

Harry laughs loudly. "I knew it!" Then he zips his lips shut. "I'll take it to my grave." Grinning widely, he then asks, "Who is it?"

Duke snorts. "That will go to *my* grave."

Harry chuckles. "You're no fun."

Duke ignores him and goes to his room as fast as his legs will carry him. The sound of his brother's laughter follows him down the hall.

Grant meets him at the door. "Milord, how was your tea?"

He growls in answer, yanking his coat off. He throws it on a nearby chair wanting to throw something else more substantial. He can be real with his manservant; it's exhausting hiding his entire life behind a persona. But not even Grant knows about his flying machine.

"I'm sorry, my Prince. I was hoping for better." Grant picks up the discarded jacket, laying it over his arm.

"You and me both, Grant. It is what it is. I can't expect miracles."

You found one just this morning. Or have you forgotten? Char's voice startles him. He hides his reaction.

Char is something he must keep hidden from even Grant, so he answers her in thought alone. 'No, I haven't. You know I cannot pursue that option.'

So, she is an option! Ha! I knew it!

Duke ignores her crowing and goes to his office, adjacent to his sitting room. "If anyone asks for me, Grant, I'm busy."

"Yes, Milord. I will be sure to chase any bothersome interruptions away."

"And no more teas. *Please.*"

"Uh, Milord, that was directly ordered by your mother. I could have done nothing to avoid that particular appointment."

Duke sighs heavily. "Yes, I know. Just ... hold everything else off. My patience is spent."

"Yes, sir."

Between his brother, the lies about his dual life, and an unhappy marriage on the horizon, Duke truly has no more energy to pretend. Settling into his leather seat, he opens the hidden compartment in his desk, pulling out the flying machine's plans. It's the only thing that settles his mind.

Duke had made the error one day of leaving them out, but Grant has, so far, not mentioned it. He can only hope Grant didn't actually see them.

He works for hours, getting lost in the details, taking meticulous notes. After studying one portion for several moments, he moans. That's going to take fingers much nimbler than his. He supposes he'll have to construct tools that will do the job for him.

Then a thought hits him so hard, he leans back in his seat, all breath whooshing out of him. Running his hands through his hair, he wonders if he could actually do what he's imagining. Smiling widely, he remembers the small fingers that poked through the window of his lair. Those are fingers he could use. Then his thoughts turned to her obvious fascination when she looked at his project. She seemed interested. How much of that could he exploit?

He ignores the twinge in his conscience. After all, she's exploiting him.

It's a good idea.

Knowing he's alone, he says aloud to Char, "You think so?" He rubs his jaw.

She would make a fantastic assistant.

"How do you know?"

I am an excellent judge of character.

"You haven't even met her."

I've seen enough through your eyes. Ask her. I do not want my beak abused in the way it was this morning. Ever again.

"You and your indignities."

My beak is for hunting and tearing into flesh for dinner, not to be used as a tool. Ask her.

"She can't know about you," he says firmly. "You are not negotiable. I need you, Char."

Then tell her about me. I'd like to meet her officially.

"No. Absolutely not."

If it wasn't for me, you wouldn't even have this opportunity! What's one more secret? Besides, she's already bound to keep all of your activities a secret. Talking to me is an activity.

"That is semantics. I can't risk it, Char."

Char is quiet a moment. *I would imagine a wife of yours would eventually find out about me.*

Duke picks his head up. "She is *not* my wife."

Duke, I am giving you permission to tell this fae woman about me. What you decide to do with that is up to you. For now, at least make her your assistant. I refuse to be used as a tool on your project.

"Fine, fine," he says, sighing, unsure if she will even return tonight so he can ask this precarious question. "She might ask for more money." But then he smiles at the thought. He rather hopes she will and that he'll get another show of her gumption.

Pay her whatever she wants.

"I understand. I'll ask her."

Be sure you do.

He can only hope he gets the same sight tonight that he's had already: her hair unbound, fire flashing in her eyes. But he will keep his precious pet a secret. Not even a bargain could convince him otherwise.

Chapter Nine

The Maid

Trudging home after a long day of laundry and serving nobles, Elora walks into her home, and is immediately assaulted with a cloying odor. She's not sure why she isn't used to the smell of illness yet.

Quickly covering her face with a large white mask set by the door, she hurries into her mother's room. The mask does the dual purpose of not contracting the contagious illness and covering rank smells.

Her heart lurches at the sight of her mother's still form shrinking as the days go by. Her mother attempts to raise her hand, but Elora says, "No, Mother, don't move. I'm here. Would you like some water?"

Her mother nods weakly. She has a mask on too, so Elora can't see her entire expression. *Is she in pain again?* Elora rushes to her bedside, filling a cup of water from the pitcher that sits next to it. She tugs the mask down and raises the cup to her mother's lips.

"Take small sips, Mother dear. That's it. We need to be sure you keep it down this time."

Her mother takes dutiful small sips, and Elora lowers the cup when she's satisfied her mother has had enough. Elora moves the mask back into place.

Just that small act seems to take a lot out of her mother. She sags against the pillow.

How much more can she take? She needs that venom now! She goes to the bowl of water and quickly washes her hands with plenty of soapwort; glad she had picked some more. It's proven invaluable to keeping the illness away from her and her father. She takes the bowl out of the room, pouring it out in the water chute.

Her father's voice interrupts her thoughts. He sounds defeated. "I wonder if the venom would even help at this point."

Elora looks up with alarm.

"She's had the illness for three months now, love, and she's lived far longer than most at her stage," he finishes with a choked sob. Holding up his arm, he covers his face with his sleeve. His shoulders shake.

"Oh, Father." Elora rushes to him and holds him. After several moments that break Elora's heart into pieces, her father stills and sighs. She releases him. "I'll go make her broth."

Elora walks into the kitchen and impulsively pulls down the raspberries and flour canister. Thanks to her father being a gardener, she had a lot more access to fresh ingredients than most servants. She retrieves the bones to make her mother's chicken broth, drops them in water to boil, then turns to the more pleasurable task of baking. Bending down, she shoots out fire from her fingers to light up the wood in the stove.

She'd bake for the prince every night for the rest of her life if it meant he could save her mother's life. Practically able to bake with her eyes closed, she falls into the familiar routine of putting the ingredients together to make mouth-watering scones.

Eyeing the apple tarts she had made in the early hours of the morning, she fights embarrassment.

Will she seem desperate? Will he suspect why she needs the money?

No, she's never mentioned her mother, and besides, she could just say she enjoys baking, which she does. And what better way to sweeten up the prince than through his stomach?

Half an hour later, the scones are baking, and she's stirring the bone broth, seasoning it with dried herbs. Her mother's stomach can't bear much, but Elora can make it a little more palatable. After another thirty minutes, she pulls the scones out of the oven, pleased with their form. She sprinkles them with sugar and decides they're ready.

She scans the sky out the window for the placement of the moon. Seeing that it's only ten o'clock, she decides she has time for a nap before she goes to meet the prince. *Will he even be in his bunker?*

Shoving all worry from her mind, she moves the bone broth to the back of the stove. She goes to let her father know she's going to bed, letting her father tend her mother tonight. She's thankful a distracted Candy agreed to take her shift again tomorrow morning. Her dear friend had been talking to a groom, and Elora used her distraction to wheedle another favor.

When she peeks in on her father, however, he's talking quietly to her mother, who seems to be sleeping. Elora often observes this scene. Her father shares about his day, whether her mother hears or not, Elora's not sure.

Not wanting to interrupt him, she takes herself to bed. She blinks to keep her eyes from drooping closed as she sets her wind-up alarm clock. Thoroughly exhausted from her night-time activities and daytime duties, she falls into bed. She's asleep as soon as her head hits the pillow.

When her alarm rings, she wakes with a start and jumps out of bed and checks the time. Seeing it's two in the morning, she rushes out of her bedroom to the kitchen and plates up the now long-cooled scones and a few of the tarts. Biting her lip, she looks over them critically. Duke seemed to love her tarts, but will he enjoy the scones, too?

Opening the door quietly, she peeks out to make sure no one is about. It's highly improbable at this hour, but she checks, nevertheless. She keeps to the shadows, staying safely out of sight. Within twenty minutes, she reaches the edge of the town near the Prince's bunker.

Her heart soars when she sees lights within. She shakes her hands out, stilling her nerves. She has to demand that she receive the money sooner rather than later. *Please, Creator, let him have some of it.*

Holding her breath, she approaches the bunker. Standing in front of the door, she takes a deep breath, building up her nerves. Before she can knock, however, the prince whips the door open. The fright almost makes her drop her plate, she presses the rim into her stomach.

He looks down at her offering, his mouth spreading in a wide smile. "You have more delectable treats? Come in, come in." Moving aside, he waits for her to pass before he looks both ways and then shuts the door.

He's at her side in the next moment, easing the plate from her stiff fingers. "Are you alright?" He crouches to look into her eyes, but she's not sure what he sees. She tries to shove the worry for her mother off her face.

She licks her lips and manages, "I'm fine. You just scared me, that's all."

"I apologize for that."

"How did you know I was at the door?" She scans the area, her eyes feasting on the massive boat-like craft on the table. She shudders at the dirt walls and floors. She feels dirty just being in this room. She has a penchant for cleanliness and it's not just that she's a maid.

He taps his ear with his finger. "I could hear you from a league away. You don't walk quietly."

She studies him. He has a look that says there's more to the story, but she drops it. She didn't monitor her steps, so he could have heard her.

He selects a scone and bites into it. Moaning with relish, he licks his lips then takes another bite, finishing it in a few mouthfuls. He looks wolfishly at her. "You might be a keeper if you continue plying me with your baking."

She walks slowly around the table, peering closely at the massive machine to see the intricate work that seems to cover the whole of one end. Some kind of metal wheels fit together like a puzzle on the outer edge, but when she moves to touch it, the prince says, "Ah, ah, ah. No touching, if you please. Unless..."

He regards her with another look she can't decipher, almost like he's taking her measure.

"Unless what?" She pulls her hand to her chest.

Instead of answering her, he looks down at the plate and picks up another scone. "What are these? Are they raspberry? Are you *trying* to make me fall in love with you?"

"Absolutely not," she blurts, a blush covering her face. "I just, uh, thought you'd like some. I do love baking, you know."

He smiles, his mouth full. But instead of offensive, she finds his antics, and clear adoration for her baking, endearing. Hiding her smile, she turns to further investigate the room.

It seems the prince does like his area tidy because she spies a broom and cleaning rags covering the surfaces of several tables. For the most part, besides a thin layer of sawdust on the boat-thing, everything seems relatively clean.

"Okay, now that I've polished off that delicious plate, we can talk business," he says brushing off his fingers, setting the plate down.

She spins at that announcement, her heart in her throat. *Does he have her money now? Has the Creator heard her prayers?*

Duke pulls out a pouch from his pants pocket, weighing it in his hand. "Seventeen hundred pounds as promised." And just like that, he holds out the pouch.

Walking carefully toward him, she pinches her arm to be sure she's not dreaming.

He watches her pinch herself and frowns. "Do you need proof that I'm not a dream? Because I can think of a much better way than hurting your arm. A much more pleasant way," he drawls.

A decidedly unladylike squeaky laugh escapes before she clamps her lips shut. "No, that's perfectly alright, the pinch was sufficient."

"No dream. This is all too real." He wiggles the pouch for her to take it.

Reaching for it, she jumps when her fingers brush his, electricity sparking. "Oh! I'm sorry."

He smirks at her. "You seem to carry a current, as if you're a spark. I think," he says slowly, "that's what I'll call you, Little Spark."

Looking into the heavy pouch, her stomach pitches at seeing wealth like she's never before held in her hands. She wants to run from the room straight to the apothecary, pound on their doors and demand they hand over vampire venom.

Barely restraining herself, she clutches the pouch to her chest. She whispers, "I didn't think you'd have this tonight." Her throat threatens to close at the powerful assurance that her mother will live a while longer now.

The prince leans against the wall, rubbing his wrist where they had made the bargain. "It's not all of what I promised. But you made a pretty powerful omission in your bargain oath, Little Spark."

She refuses to allow her heart to warm to his endearment. She finds she doesn't mind the nickname. Although, he probably gives every fae woman one. She nods toward his arm. "The bargain is making you aware you haven't completed it, isn't it? It lets me know when I've struck too close to mentioning my time with you, too. And I know I didn't specify a time. I realized that after I left, that I didn't say when you need to pay the, uh, sum.

But I need it quickly, Prince." There, she said it. She twists her apron in her fidgety hands. She bites her lip.

Pushing against the dirt wall, he stands tall again. "You're going to need to give me some time. I may need to give it to you in batches." He rubs his arm again, wincing.

"How much time?" Her mind spins wondering how a bunch of small doses will affect her mother and if it will even work to heal her.

Shaking his head, he straightens. "I can probably produce the coin within a few months." He bends over, cradling his arm. "Ahhhhh, that stings."

"A few *months*?" Her heart speeds up with fear coursing through her.

He stands up, walking toward her, shaking his hand out. "Are you in some kind of trouble? Are you in danger?"

She licks her lips, thinking through how to word her mother's dire predicament without mentioning her. "I can't tell you much, only that someone I care about will die if I can't get my hands on that money, the full amount, within the month."

"That, my dear," he winces, "is going to be a problem."

Chapter Ten

The Prince

"**I** don't know how much money you assume I personally possess, but…" Duke falters. "It's going to take time to get my hands on that kind of money."

"I don't *have* time!" Tears well up in Elora's eyes, and she turns around. "You're the *Prince Heir*. If anyone could get it, it's *you*."

He rubs the back of his neck, trying to figure out how he could possibly fulfill the bargain within the month. He shakes his head. If he asks his mother for that much all at once, she'll crack down on him even more than she is now, thinking he needs firm guidance with his spending. She'll assume he's gambling it all away. He does not want any more of her attention on him.

But, hearing Elora's quiet sobs, makes him want to take that chance even more than wanting the burning in his arm to stop. Stepping toward her, he asks gently, "What were you going to do before our clandestine meeting? If you'd never discovered my secret life here?"

She sobs into her hand. Her reply is muffled. "I was going to say goodbye to her. I had made peace with it. But now with hope so close, I can't help but think..."

So, it's a woman.

Duke nods at Char's words and strokes his chin. He thinks back, 'And the money is for a cure of some kind.'

I would bet anything it's for vampire venom. They set those vials at exorbitant prices.

He agrees. What would be easier: procuring vampire venom or another 3300 pounds? He blows out a breath. Both tasks seem impossible.

Clearing his throat, he throws out an idea. "I could always ask my brother for a loan."

Elora spins around, her golden eyes shining fervently. The effect is mesmerizing.

"But I'll need at least a month," he says firmly.

She nods so hard the kerchief holding her hair comes loose and falls to the floor. Mercy. If she keeps loosing her hair like that, he'll promise her the moon. Stooping to pick up the soft piece of fabric, he says, "Here, pull yourself together. Everything is going to be fine. I'll ... I'll figure something out."

"I'll bake for you every day," she gushes, reaching for her cloth. Almost impatiently, she ties her hair back. "Anything you want, I'll make it for you."

At her luminous eyes, he's struck silent.

"I can make chocolate croissants, pies, cakes, any sweets you want." Taking his silence as something negative, she continues, "And...and if you need any kind of cleaning around here," she looks around the space. "Or anywhere, I'll be happy to clean. I mean, I'll start right now." She pockets the coin pouch in her skirt and dashes toward a cleaning cloth. Snatching it up, she starts scrubbing the first table she sees.

"I'll work day and night, do anything you ask, just please," she falters, pausing after taking a shaking breath. "Please help me." Then she resumes her frantic work, a tear dropping off her nose and onto the table.

Shaken loose from his temporary paralysis, he walks toward her, taking the cloth from her grasp gently, and holding her hands. "Listen to me," he says quietly.

When she tries to tug her hands free, fresh tears spill down her cheeks. "You don't understand."

"I do. I do understand," he says in a deep, low voice.

She stops her struggle and looks up at him with tentative hope. "You do?"

He nods. "I think I understand completely. Now stop this infernal cleaning, Little Spark. As entertaining as it is to see how quickly you move, I need your help in another way."

Her forehead wrinkles. "My help? All I know how to do is bake and clean."

He stifles a grin. She's so adorable even when she looks lost. She's yanked on his heartstrings with the care she feels for the sick woman in her life. Vampire venom is known to cure all kinds of ills. "I actually find myself in need of an assistant."

She looks towards the flying machine. This time when she tugs on her hands, he lets them go. She wipes her face free of tears. "Assist you with this creation? Truly?"

He tucks his hands in his pockets to prevent himself from reaching for her again. Her small hands felt so good in his. "As a matter of fact, yes."

"But I haven't the faintest notion of how to help you," she says faintly.

"I'll teach you."

"You will?" A look of wonder crosses her face as her head swings to the flying machine.

He nods, drinking in her every expression. He's so used to noble fae who suppress their feelings and rarely let them show. Elora's spectrum of emotion is enchanting.

Forcing himself to walk toward his machine, he casually picks up a screwdriver, twirling it around his fingers. "Does this arrangement sound agreeable?"

She barks a short laugh. "Are you kidding? I'd love to learn about this ... boat, or thing you're working on. Can you tell me what it is now?" She walks slowly around the table, much like she did the first time she saw his project, studying it with apparent fascination.

"It's a flying machine. Or it will be. One day. Hopefully."

From behind the table, she looks up at him, her mouth in an open O. "Truly? You'll be able to fly in this?"

He chuckles, running his hand through his hair. "That's the idea. I have much more work to do first."

She breathes out a sigh. "I admit, it would be a marvel if you could manage it. Is there anything like this in all of Lurin?"

Duke shakes his head. "Not that I know of. I've kept my ears open for a machine like this but haven't heard of anything. There have been prototypes, of course. But they've all failed."

Tilting her head to one side, she says, "Tell me about them."

Duke smiles, happy to talk about this with someone other than Char. "The only flying machines I've heard of are more along the lines of gliders. Nothing with a mechanical engine to make it fly. Gliders rely on the wind patterns. Which, this will have to adjust to, of course, but with my design, will fly on its own."

She laughs. "It sounds like a miracle."

His eyes linger on the pleasure of her smile. It brightens her entire face, lighting up her golden eyes and bringing a rosiness to her cheeks.

He pauses to get his thoughts together. She's scrambled every word in his head. She looks at him curiously. She must be wondering why he's staring at her so. He manages to say, "A lot of it will be a product of the Creator's will, but no, this is more science than miracle. But I certainly need the Creator's help."

She nods and peers inside the hull. "So, is this where you'll sit?"

"Yes, the pilot will sit there."

"Surely, it will be you showing off this beauty," she casually remarks.

His heart warms at her praise but then clenches at having to keep his identity a secret. "I will wear a disguise when I demonstrate how it works."

She spins around, her long skirts swirling. "Why would you do that?"

"I'm supposed to be a prince, not an inventor." He shrugs, trying to look like he doesn't care.

She cocks her head and puts her hands on her hips. "That's terrible. There shouldn't be any doubt who built this."

Changing the subject, he says, "Well, I wouldn't trust anyone else to fly it, anyway. Not until I'm sure of its success."

She nods. "Of course. That is imperative."

"I wouldn't want anyone's death on my conscience."

"No," she says quietly, instantly sobering.

Again, he wonders who it is she's trying to save. He decides to wait until she trusts him more before asking.

"So, do we have a deal?" he asks, holding his breath.

Elora looks up at him, biting her lip yet again. "We don't have to make another bargain if I agree, do I?"

He chuckles, tearing his eyes away from her delectable little habit. "No, Little Spark. I will be happy with a verbal agreement."

She breathes out a sigh of relief. "Well then, I agree. I'll be your assistant for the next month." She straightens.

Duke's stomach clenches. Taking only a month to complete the intricate work will be difficult. He won't force her to do anything more than what she's willing, though.

They have enough on their heads, or rather, wrists, as it is. She's already bound to keep his true self a secret. He can't ask for more.

I wouldn't say that. Everything is negotiable.

'No, Char. One month will have to be enough.'

We'll see.

No, if there's one thing he prides himself on, it's the value of his word. He'll just have to get as much of the detailed work done while he has Elora's assistance. Or, rather, his Little Spark.

He smiles to himself. If only he had known what she would be doing for him. She's the spark that will get his machine to fly.

How could he have lived with this woman in the periphery of his life for years and failed to notice her inspiring spirit?

Getting to work, he finds he doesn't have an answer to that but is happy he can flesh it out now.

Chapter Eleven

The Maid

Elora slips into her home and listens at her mother's door to make sure she's settled. Satisfied she's sleeping comfortably, Elora falls into bed without even changing out of her clothes.

As her body relaxes into the soft bedding, she remembers the prince looking startled when her kerchief fell off. It's like the idea of her hair loose scares him, and for some reason that makes her smile as she drifts off to sleep.

Waking up after the sun, she's thankful to have switched shifts with Candy because her mother needs her. Her father was trying to feed her a breakfast of simple bone broth, but her mother's stomach couldn't keep it down.

She rushes in to help when her father looks lost as he tries to clean her mother up. Elora shoos him off to work and does the task herself. After her mother is as settled as she can be, Elora has just enough time to rush to the apothecary before her duties at the castle.

The chemist, Pat, frowns when he looks up to find Elora walking into his shop. She and her father have exhausted every affordable remedy for her mother, so his frown doesn't surprise her. The fact that Pat hasn't turned their family in is a testament to his compassion. They've never told him her mother suffers from the wasting illness, but she's certain he's guessed. Looking around the shop, she's thankful to be his only client. She walks up to the counter.

"Elora, dear. I'm afraid I have nothing more to give you," he says in a gravelly voice. He resumes pouring liquid into small vials with a troubled frown.

She leans in and says, "Actually, you do, Pat."

He looks up at her. "You know the only remedy left. And I can't give it away."

"I know," she says, reaching into her pocket.

When he sees her lift the heavy pouch of coin and put it on his counter, he stops what he's doing and whispers, looking all around, "Where did you get this, Child?"

"I cannot say, sir. But please examine it. There's enough there for a small vial of the venom."

His brows furrow as he picks up the pouch and spills the coin on the counter. After he's finished counting it, he says quietly, "Child, I worry for you, I truly do. This is a large sum. But for your mother to recover completely, you'll need much more than this can buy."

"I am aware, sir." Elora's chest pinches at his words. She had known this, but to hear it spoken isn't easy to accept.

Shaking his head, he gathers the money, but before he puts it away, he asks in a grave tone, "Elora, are you sure you want to spend this in this way? It would give your mother three weeks at most."

She nods amid fresh tears, and swallows hard, stammering, "I—I understand." She holds onto her faith in the prince — that he will come through with the rest of the money in time. She takes a deep, shaky breath.

Sighing heavily, he lumbers his large form to the money drawer, depositing the coin into it. Elora eyes him, knowing she'd give every last bit she had to have more time with her frail mother.

Then he turns and goes into the back of the shop, emerging with a vial so small, Elora wonders if it's the right medicine. That's all that the prince's coin paid for?

"Would you like me to wrap this?" he asks, eyeing her intently.

He's asking if she wants him to hide her purchase. And the answer is yes, absolutely.

She nods in two short movements.

He takes a nondescript cloth and wraps the tiny vial in it. Just then, a neighbor walks into the apothecary. Elora's eyes widen at the chemist, but he continues as if nothing interesting were happening.

Elora holds her breath when she realizes he hasn't explained how to administer this life-saving medication. Her heart pounds and her hands sweat. She tries to keep her eyes on Pat.

"Now," he says, after flicking a glance at the neighbor before focusing back on Elora. "Administer this with tea or by itself for best potency. Come back with any questions."

Elora is bursting with questions, but she can't ask them just now. Thanking the chemist, she gives a thin-lipped smile to her neighbor and escapes out the door, clutching the cloth-wrapped treasure.

She rushes home so fast, she nearly trips several times. She dares not run and risk falling and breaking the vial. Elora keeps her eyes on the ground, so she doesn't have to talk to anyone she passes. She passes several treehouses before reaching hers. Since they're on the first floor, she doesn't have to pass anyone on the stairs. Finally reaching her door, she bursts in.

Pressing her lips together, she takes a deep breath and removes the tiny vial from her pocket. Unwrapping the cloth, she fingers the wax that seals the cork stopper in place. She takes a moment to peel it off. Biting her lip, she agonizes over administering the dose correctly. Should she pour it down her mother's throat? What if she chokes it all up? No, she'll give it to her in measured doses in tea, slowly so her stomach will accept it.

Uncorking the miniscule bottle, she carefully pours every bit of the venom into some tea beside her mother's bed, stirring it with a spoon.

Please, Creator, let this heal my mother. Give us more time with her.

Elora doesn't want to have to wake her mother, and she sags in relief when she sees her mother already awake. She blinks, having lost the energy to talk some days ago.

Elora sets the cup carefully down and props her mother's head up, saying softly, "Mother, dear, if you can, please drink this tea very slowly. It's very, very important that you keep it all down. It's vampire venom, Mother. I actually got some. You need to drink every drop."

Her mother's eyes cloud over in confusion, then they sharpen with some clarity. They widen and then swing over to the cup. She gives a barely discernable nod, and Elora wastes no time in holding the cup to her mother's cracked lips.

Small sips sound in the room, and Elora prays the entire time. She gives her mother a break after she drinks half of the tea. "How does that feel, Mother? Can you drink some more in a few moments?"

Already some color returns to her mother's pale cheeks, and Elora blinks quickly to be sure she hasn't imagined it. Her mother nods a little more firmly and fastens her gaze on the tea Elora holds carefully in her hands.

Feeling emboldened and hoping she's not making a mistake in rushing the medication into her, she returns the cup to her mother's lips.

She swallows more this time, and Elora says, "Mother, not so fast. It's important you keep this down." She slowly drinks it, however, and then with a sigh, her head falls back to the pillow.

She's out in moments, and Elora relaxes when she sees her mother's chest rise and fall in steady breaths. Leaning down, she looks more closely at her mother's face.

There's a soft pink to her cheeks, which makes Elora's heart sing. She sets the empty cup on the bedside table. She's already late for her shift at the palace. Though she desperately wants to stay home to keep watch for any changes, she forces herself to leave.

A timid hope soars through her as she hurries to the palace. Then worry replaces it. Will her mother keep the medicine down? Her father won't be home for hours yet. If she gets sick, no one is home to care for her.

Desperately needing her job at the palace, she finishes her walk and goes around the back to the kitchens. They're placed at the bottom of the palatial tree house and occupy the entire first floor of the enormous structure. As soon as she enters the door, she hears Paula yelling at the top of her voice. "Where is that worthless friend of yours, Candy? She's late!"

Hurrying her way in, she passes Candy, who gives her a worried look. With an apology already on her lips, Elora implores, "I'm so very sorry, Mistress Paula. I had a very good reason, I assure you. It will not happen again."

Paula's eagle eyes scrutinize her. "And what good reason do you have, Child?"

Chafing at being called a child at her adult eighteen years, she bites back a retort and answers, "My mother was not feeling well, Mistress. I aided her."

Paula harrumphs. "This is the second time I've heard that excuse. What is your mother's malady?"

Elora's heart pounds, and her mouth dries. Swallowing, she fumbles for an excuse. "She suffers from a lingering cough."

Paula frowns deeply. "Yes, well, as long as it isn't the wasting illness. Be sure you're not late again or you'll be out of a job, young lady."

Elora nods. "I'll begin my duties right away. Again, forgive me." She can't help but feel Paula's suspicious stare on her back as she reaches for a bin of potatoes she needs to peel.

She wills her hands to stop trembling and begins her chore, praying for the safety of her mother until the full remedy can be obtained. As she works, she adds another prayer to her list of requests: that the Prince can procure the full amount before it's too late.

Chapter Twelve

The Prince

Duke lounges on the couch in the full drawing room, itching to leave and do what he truly loves. Alas, that's not an option for hours. He pulls at his tight cravat. He's already suffered through another tea with three fae women earlier today, and his patience is stretched painfully thin. If only he could recover those hours of his life, he would gladly take them. He still has dinner to endure and then brandy afterward.

Looking over the brightly lit room, he vaguely wonders about the number of lamps in use; it looks like a hundred or more. They bring the elaborate drawing room into stark wonder, boasting finely made chairs and tables. Fae nobles meander around, dressed in fine suits and elaborate dresses. He hides a grimace. They're all talking, sipping cocktails, and working the room, pushing their own social agendas. He knows he's supposed to be out there with them, but he has no interest in talking about inane things. Instead, he focuses his mind on the intricate work of the flying machine's engine.

He's lost in nuts and bolts when Char says, *I'm in almost as much pain as you are just listening to your thoughts. Must you always think of that contraption?*

'What I would give for something interesting to happen. Maybe you could fly through the room while wearing your flames?'

I would love to distract you from your perch on that comfortable couch, oh Indolent One, but I value my life, thank you very much.

Duke shudders at the thought of one of the guards posted at the door unleashing their arrows on his precious friend.

He wishes for nothing other than his underground bunker and enduring Char's wit. He's surrounded by opulence, but he can't bring himself to care. Elora flits through his thoughts as a welcome distraction.

I am *much better company than these simpletons. So is she for that matter.*

Char is the one thing that makes his time during these events bearable. He can always count on her sharp repertoire of comments. It's taken time to mask his facial reactions to her often hilarious observations, but he's learned to do so over the two years they've been mind-melded.

'What would I do without you, my dear friend?'

You'd die of boredom.

'Probably.'

The Creator knew what He was doing by bringing us together.

"Were you listening, dear Prince?" A voice interrupts his inner conversation.

Duke looks over at Lady Mary, who stands, hands on hips, a few feet away. He hadn't noticed her at all. "I'm sorry, Lady Mary, what did you say? My mind was wandering."

She opens her fan and snaps it closed. "Oh, it's of no bother, Prince." She presses her rouge-stained lips together in a thin line.

Duke resists rolling his eyes. The language of the fan speaks more loudly about her true feelings than her words.

Char laughs loudly in his head. *Doesn't that little fan trick mean that you're cruel? Oh, that's rich. If she only knew how you really felt.*

"What did you say, dear Lady Mary?" He leans forward in his seat in an act of feigned sincerity.

Seeming encouraged, she repeats, "Are you escorting anyone to the Midnight Ball?" She blinks slowly at him, acting coy.

Duke looks away. He acted too well to inspire such a question. That ball is months away. And he knows she's hinting at accompanying him, but he's going to have to disappoint her yet again. "I do not have the pleasure of escorting a lovely lady—"

"Oh, I'm avail—"

"And I'm not going to."

She deflates. "Oh." And there goes her fan opening and snapping closed again.

Lady Elizabeth chooses that moment to join their conversation. "Hello Prince, how are you this evening?"

He dutifully smiles at her. "I'm well, Lady Elizabeth."

"Did I interrupt?" She looks at her sister, concern marring her brow at the slight scowl Lady Mary disguises behind her fan.

Wanting to cushion his rather rude remark to her sister, he says, "We were discussing the Midnight Ball. And you see, Lady Mary," he says, directing his attention to her. "There's a shortage of fae ladies to pair up with the gentlemen that evening. I wouldn't dream of robbing the eligible men of delightful dates."

Char cackles. *Oh, that's rich. What a good politician you are.*

'I am the fae prince. I must be.' He thinks with a straight face.

Lady Elizabeth smiles primly. "How very magnanimous of you, Prince, to be so considerate." A fae man approaches her and pulls her attention away.

Lady Mary rallies, looking toward the open doors letting in the night air. "Well, it is a delightful evening. I'd love to see the view from the balcony. I'm sure we could have a … lovely time together, out there alone."

Duke adjusts in his seat uncomfortably. He's often put in compromising situations with women who would do anything to become queen. He has no desire to be in such a situation tonight. So, he pulls the social card that trumps all else. "Uh, I'm sorry, my dear, but I see my mother needs me."

Out of the frying pan and into the fire.

Ignoring Char's unhelpful comment, Duke bids farewell to Lady Mary and eases off the couch, walking sedately toward his mother. She's reigning over the court from her place next to his father in the middle of the room. As this is an informal evening, she's not on a throne, but the seat she's on mimics one perfectly.

The queen sits with perfectly straight posture in a high-backed chair with hand-carved scrollwork that must have taken an artisan weeks to complete. Her chair is identical to his father's. When Duke approaches, she subtly turns her head, acknowledging him with a nod before returning her attention to her conversation.

With his mother busy, he turns to his father, who's watching over the conversations, currently not speaking to anyone. "Father, I trust you are having a pleasant evening?"

The King shifts his large form around on the chair and gives him his full attention. "I see you were speaking to the Lady Mary just now."

"Yes, I was. She's a delightful woman."

His father gives a small snort. "She can't be that delightful if you ran away from her."

Duke holds back a cringe.

Into the fire, like I said.

"Well, I, uh, thought I saw mother calling for me." He tries to buy into his own lie.

The king gives Duke a knowing smile. "Son, you can't give that excuse every time you wish to escape a conversation."

Opting for honesty, he says in a low voice, "Father, she was asking for an intimate moment on the balcony."

The king's eyebrow rises. "Was she? That's quite daring. They're getting bolder and bolder these days." He sighs, his jowls trembling and taps his finger on his knee. Duke wishes his father would come down from the lofty heights of the tree house and use the stairs, then he would get some exercise and lose some of his hefty weight. "If she hasn't caught your attention, have any of these fine women done so?"

Instantly, the vision of Elora with her hair cascading all around her fills his mind.

His father chuckles. "I see someone has."

Duke masks his face with a blank expression. "No, Father, I don't think so."

The king purses his lips, looking thoughtfully over the crowd of mingling nobles. "I was rather hoping you'd choose your future queen soon, my son. I'm not getting any younger, and I'd like to meet my grandchildren before I die."

"Father, don't say such a thing. You have many, many years yet." Duke sweats under the tight knots at his neck.

"What is he saying now, my son?" the Queen asks, her conversation finished.

Duke licks his lips, suddenly parched. "He's talking nonsense, Mother."

His father clears his throat, straightening in his chair. "It's nonsense to talk of your upcoming marriage and my progeny? I'd like to give you the crown in the next couple of years. You'll need to be married by then."

"Oh? What marriage? Have you finally chosen a life mate?" the Queen asks, her voice cutting, even though she speaks softly so they're not overheard.

Duke's chest tightens. "*No*, Mother," Duke says, running his hand over his face. "Father mentioned his death, which I objected to."

"What is this?" Queen Alexandria says, leaning back to peer at her husband. "What nonsense is he speaking of?"

"Duke," the king hisses. "Do not alarm your mother so. You have a duty to marry and have heirs, and I have every right to remind you of it. Just because I said I'd like to meet my grandchildren before I die does not mean I'm to keel over this very evening."

With a direct gaze at Duke, his mother says, "Your father's perfectly right. It's high time you chose your future queen. We have been patient enough."

Is the fire getting hotter, dear Prince?

Duke ignores Char's laughter and shifts on his feet. Maybe he made the wrong choice in coming over here. He should have risked the balcony.

He's saved when his brother walks up. "What delightful conversation am I interrupting? Father looks like he's ready to have an apoplexy."

Duke glares at Harry but glances at his father. Indeed, his face is bright red.

The queen says, "We were discussing marriage, my dear son. Your brother is being quite frustrating concerning the topic. Would you happen to know which of these fine ladies has caught his eye?" She nods her head around the room.

That's a low blow. Asking your brother to tell on you.

Forcing his face not to show any alarm at what his brother could reveal, Duke says in a low voice, "Mother, isn't this topic best discussed in a more private setting?"

She turns her eagle gaze to his. "I would do so, Son, if I didn't have to force answers out of you."

He sighs. "I have found no one of romantic interest, Mother." A wild idea of how he could delay his mother's matchmaking plans strikes his mind. "Maybe it's because the pickings here are so slim. Let's invite the entire fae kingdom to the Midnight Ball so I may entertain all options."

The queen raises her eyebrow. "Would you truly like that? To invite all the fae noble ladies to the ball? I can see merit in that, I suppose. If I do, will you choose your bride?"

"I know *I* would like that," Harry says in a jovial voice. He slaps Duke's shoulder. "You have all the best ideas."

Duke delivers a grim smile to his grinning brother, feeling like a noose has come around his neck, tightening. He pulls on his cravat. He turns back to his mother. "Yes, sometime soon. I'm quite looking forward to the prospect."

"Wedding prospects, you mean, Duke?" Harry asks, his eyes bright with mirth.

"Duke," his mother says in sharp tone. "No more dilly dallying. I'm giving you until the Midnight Ball to choose a bride or I will choose one for you. And I'm moving the date up. It'll be in one month."

Duke breaks out in a cold sweat when her gaze flits to the Strafford sisters.

"That won't be necessary, Mother." His blood pounds heavy in his veins. And why is Elora's face the only one he envisions standing beside him as queen? That's impossible. She's a maid, not a noble lady.

The queen nods then waves him away. "Go on with your brother, Duke, dear. I need to speak with my courtiers of this grand idea of yours. They will be in an exceptional uproar about inviting all the fae ladies in the land for your hand in marriage."

He barely manages to stifle a groan when he drags his brother by the arm. "We need to talk," he hisses. Like putting his head in the sand, he's going to try to forget his mother's ridiculous demand. Instead, he'll focus on what he has control of.

Chuckling, Harry allows himself to be led to a more private corner. "What rebuke could you possibly want to burn my ears with?"

Looking around to be sure no one approaches, Duke says in a low voice, "You could have outed your suspicions to our dear mother. I owe you for keeping your mouth shut. But first I must owe you much more."

Harry cocks his head. "What's this? I'm dying of curiosity. First, you suggest a Nebraria-wide ball. Now, you're offering to owe *me*?"

Duke leans in and spits out, "I need money. A lot of it."

Surprise replaces his brother's amused expression. "*You* need money? Isn't that what I usually ask for? What mess have you gotten yourself into?"

Duke blows out a breath. "I can't say. But I need to get my hands on thirty-three hundred pounds in a month." His wrist burns in warning, as if to hurry Duke up.

Harry rears back as if he's been struck. He whistles lowly, his eyes widening. "Truly?"

"I'm afraid so."

And you're counting on your imbecile of a brother for this? Duke!

Duke ignores Char's heated words.

Harry looks around the room, as if he could find answers to his burning questions there. He returns his gaze back to Duke, looking at him as if for the first time. "I find myself shocked. That's quite a sum."

"I know." He purposely avoids rubbing his arm. Harry could suspect something about his bargain.

Harry leans back on his heels. "Since I'm the one usually begging you for coin, what makes you think I have it?"

He won't.

"I'm desperate." An image of Elora's tear-filled eyes springs to his mind.

"You must be to come to me." Harry rubs his mouth, then chuckles lightly. He shakes his head. "I don't have it. Nor will I."

Am I surprised?

A courtier passes by, and Duke adopts a bored expression until he's out of earshot. "What about vampire venom? Do you have any of that?"

Char's laughing fills his ears.

Harry laughs, then, recovering quickly, quiets. He leans in to whisper. "*Vampire venom*? Why in the world do you need that?"

Impatient, Duke snaps, "I just do. Could you get some?"

Holding both hands over his mouth, Harry blows out a deep breath, then finally nods. "I actually do have a source for that."

"Is it real venom?" Duke eyes his brother intently.

Harry presses his lips together and draws down his eyebrows. "Think what you want of me, Brother, but I would never give you anything less than the real thing. The real question is this: who do you know who's ill?"

"No one you know," Duke says, then to himself, "Nor I, either."

Harry cracks a small smile. "You're becoming more and more mysterious. Vampire venom? Call me intrigued."

"I'll call you anything you want as long as you can get me that medicine." Duke knows that for the purpose of the bargain, he could take the course of his lifetime to pay Elora, since no time was specified. But he can't bring himself to face her despair if he can't help her at all. He's more than sure that's why she needs the money.

"Am I correct to assume you need it soon?" Harry asks grimly.

Duke nods. "Within the month. Sooner, if possible." When two fae women approach the princes, he's forced to say in the corner of his mouth, "Now do I need to ask you to keep this quiet?"

Harry has just enough time to say, "No, of course not," before they're face to face with the women.

When the room erupts with furious whispering, he knows his mother has spread hints of Duke finding a bride by the night of the ball. He groans. If he thought the women were forward before this knowledge, they'll be insatiable now. He'll spend the rest of the night dodging questions on who he's escorting to the grand event.

Finally, the queen rises to her feet to leave for dinner. The room follows suit. He doesn't understand why they eat so late at night. It's nearly ten o'clock, but he suffers through the meal, planning his evening's work in his mind as he makes mindless conversation with his dinner partners, who both, unsurprisingly, are eligible fae women. He dodges several requests for outings from each one.

Focusing on what he did accomplish, acquiring venom for Elora, now she can concentrate on helping him with the flying machine. Despite the looming Midnight Ball hanging over his head, he can at least enjoy his favorite pastime, which now includes a certain honey-gold haired woman.

Chapter Thirteen

The Maid

Elora takes a brief moment in the afternoon to check on her mother. She finds her sleeping comfortably, which does much to ease her mind. In the full light of the afternoon shining into the room, Elora confirms that her mother truly does look better. She has color in her cheeks for the first time in weeks.

Elora returns to her duties for the late afternoon and early evening shift, floating on a cloud of relief and joy.

When her duties finally complete for the day, Elora rushes home and finds her father talking quietly to her mother in their room. After quickly putting on her mask, she rushes into the room, exclaiming, "Mother, how are you?" She hadn't exchanged words with her for days now. She drops to a kneeling position next to the bed.

Her mother licks her lips and smiles softly. "I am well, Child."

Elora can't hold in her sobs, and she bends her head, finally breaking after watching her mother grow worse these past weeks. She had been trying to hold on, to be strong, not only for herself but for her father, as well. He rises and stands behind her, holding onto her shaking shoulders, squeezing them. Elora wipes her eyes impatiently, not wanting to waste this time with her mother.

She looks up. "I've missed you. So much."

"I know. I'm sorry I've been so ill."

"No," Elora cries, swiping her cheeks again with the back of her hand. "Don't apologize. Not for one moment."

"How did you find the venom, my dear?" her mother asks softly. Her gentle look probes Elora's heart.

"Yes, Elora, I too would very much like to hear that answer," her father says, moving back to his seat next to her mother. His sharp eyes examine her.

"Uh, well. I can't say." She falters for a moment. "But I came by it honestly, or sort of honestly. I didn't steal it," she rushes to say. "Just know I can get more."

"Daughter," her father's gravelly voice projects stark concern. "It is concerning that you've put yourself in what are obviously questionable circumstances."

"Oh, Elora. What have you done?" her mother gently chides.

"Nothing! The situation is perfectly safe, I assure you. I can't explain and please don't ask me to. I'm not in any danger, I promise you both. I'm working for it." Her wrist flares hot in warning.

His father exchanges a concerned look with his wife and then turns to Elora. "We've always trusted you, and we will continue to, but Elora, if you need aid, please ask."

Elora nods, ignoring the burning. "I will, Father. Now, Mother, tell us how you're feeling." Desperate to hold her mother's hand, she squeezes her own hands together instead. She can't touch her without her gloves.

Her mother sighs deeply. "It's like I've emerged from a powerful dream. Your father says I'd worsened over the past week, but I have no memory of it."

Elora is more than relieved that her mother doesn't remember any of the past week. It was not pleasant. She nods at her mother, encouraging her to continue.

"I'm feeling more energized, and I was able to have two cups of soup today already."

Elora looks at her father for confirmation, and he nods at her. "She did wonderfully," he says gruffly.

Tears leak from Elora's eyes, and she immediately thinks of the prince, who is the entire reason her mother has improved so dramatically. She can't wait to thank him. She just needs to be very careful she doesn't reveal that the wasting illness is in her home.

"Jane, dear, you're looking spent from visiting with us, so why don't you rest?" her father says in a soft voice.

Elora wants to spend hours talking to her mother like they used to, but she gets up, knowing her father is right.

Mother closes her eyes, and Elora leaves the room with one last lingering look behind her. Her father joins her in the kitchen.

Tears glisten in his eyes. "It's a miracle, truly, how well the venom works."

Stepping up, Elora wraps her arms around her father's trim waist and squeezes. Breathing in his earthy scent, she allows herself to enjoy the moment. Her mother is resting peacefully in the next room, her father's steady heartbeat thrums in rhythm under her ear. His heart had been giving him palpitations these past few months from all this stress. But all is well in the world.

Now, to get her hands on the rest of the money.

For the rest of the evening, she hopes and prays the prince has found a way to fulfill the rest of the bargain. Like the night before, she takes a nap to get ready for her late night. She's going to start helping him with his flying machine, and she wants to be energized for it.

Elora wakes up around two in the morning with her winding alarm and, after ensuring her mother is resting comfortably, she leaves for the bunker.

As she walks to meet the prince, she sees a flash of orange and red fly into the trees. She dashes toward the wooded area and searches up in the trees for another look.

She gasps when she spots the most beautiful bird she's ever seen sitting on a large tree branch. The bird watches her approach and doesn't break eye contact. Elora's eyes move over its large form and even larger tail with long red and orange feathers draping over the branch. It blinks at her, and Elora rubs her eyes to make sure she's not imagining the sight.

"You're gorgeous," Elora breathes, not wanting to scare the rare bird. She swears it nods, but that can't be. Now that she's studying it, she can see it's definitely a phoenix. She doesn't want to be the reason the forest burns down. If she startles the bird, it might burst into flames.

Backing away slowly, Elora keeps her eyes on it, hungrily drinking in every detail she can see. It stays on its perch watching her walk the whole way to the bunker.

She finally turns away when she arrives at the hidden workshop. Knocking softly on the door, she jumps when the prince opens it.

Pulling his arm, she yanks him out the door.

He recovers from his surprise and allows her to pull him out onto the path. "Well, hello to you, too, Little Spark."

"Shhh, don't say that!" she whispers furiously, her heart stopping. "You might give it ideas."

He chuckles as she drags him to the wooded area where she saw the bird. "Give what ideas?"

Looking everywhere for the bird, she sees only the empty branch. "Where did it go?"

"What are you talking about?" He looks at her then around the area with questioning eyes.

"I swear I saw a phoenix. It was just here! It's unbelievable ..." Scanning all the trees, she sees no sign of it. Deflated, she turns to the prince, who's frowning deeply.

"Did you say a phoenix?" He's quiet for a moment with a strange expression on his face. Why does he look frustrated?

"Yes! You have to promise not to hurt it if you see it." She grabs his arm. It's tense under her hand.

"Oh, I'll be sure to wring its neck if I see it." He scowls.

"No! Please don't, Prince. It didn't have a bit of fire on it."

The prince shakes his head. "I won't promise anything." He stalks back to the bunker, grumbling under his breath.

With one last look around, Elora follows him, feeling rather special for having glimpsed such an elusive bird.

When they enter the prince's work area, Elora sighs happily. "I've never seen such a gorgeous bird in all my life." She looks out the window trying to catch another glimpse.

The prince only continues to grumble.

Not catching his words, Elora turns around, disappointed. "It looked right at me, and I swear it nodded at me when I said it was gorgeous."

Duke only frowns and turns to his tools, roughly yanking a stool up to the table. He drops into his seat. "You shouldn't have talked to it."

"Why?" Elora walks up to him, loosening the kerchief that holds her hair. Leaning back, she shakes out her hair, sighing in relief at the immediate release of tension in her neck from the weight of her hair.

When she notices the prince looking blankly at her with his mouth open, she asks, "What is it?"

His eyes trail over her tresses that fall around her shoulders. He visibly swallows. "Uh, it's nothing." He shifts in his seat and focuses his attention on the flying machine.

Wondering why her hair makes the prince look so visibly unsettled, she hides a smile and runs her fingers through it. "Why shouldn't I have talked to the phoenix, Prince?"

He glances at her before pulling his gaze away. "You'll only encourage her. And call me Duke."

"Wait," Elora says, freezing her movements. "You know it's a female? How do you know that?" She leans toward him.

He pauses for a moment, shutting his eyes briefly. "It's just a guess," he says gruffly.

Elora sinks onto a bench. "A girl phoenix. How adorable would that be? She could have little phoenix babies." Folding her arms around her middle, she squeezes herself in delight at the thought.

Duke visibly shudders. "Please. Can we not talk about this? I have much on my mind." His face sets in a scowl.

"Okay," Elora says slowly, wondering why he looks so distressed. She hopes he won't be annoyed all evening. That will not make for good working conditions. His frown eases as he studies his work. Suddenly curious about the project at hand, she looks closer at the contraption. Taking in all the intricate details, she scoots her seat closer.

A conglomerate of metal gears and tiny metal pieces fits together in a somewhat magical arrangement. They all sit on the front of the flying machine behind the two boards that when she touches them, spins. As foreign as everything looks to her, she knows each piece has a specific function. Even so, as many pieces are in the elaborate construction, a hundred more lie all around on the table.

"Okay, so what do I do? What is all this stuff?"

Duke looks distracted, but he focuses his attention first on his work and then on Elora. "Well, first of all. It's not stuff. Each piece has a name. For instance, this entire area on the front is called an engine."

"An en-john?"

He shakes his head. "En-juhn. It's what will make this whole thing fly. Well, combined with the aerodynamical function of the shape, of course."

Elora nods, drinking in what he's saying. "Oh, of course."

He glances at her, then away. "Now, I'll be working next on the hydraulic system, which will require nimble fingers. It's rather good luck you're here to help me with that."

Elora blushes at that comment. Her blackmailing him had nothing to do with luck, but she's not going to tell him that.

He continues, pointing out a small, toothed wheel. "So, look at this particular part. See how when I move one piece, it starts a cycle of movement?"

He's so intent on what he's showing her, she's distracted for a moment at his handsome profile. When she doesn't answer, he looks quickly at her. "Elora?"

"Yes? I mean, yes, I see it." Blushing furiously, she stares at the spot he's pointing at, willing her cheeks to stop burning.

He resumes. "I'll add tubing that will flush the entire engine with oil, keeping the temperature of the engine down."

His words send a spark of interest through her. She asks, "How will it do that? It cools down the engine? All on its own? That sounds like a magical fluid."

"No," he says, flashing her an appreciative smile. "It will redistribute the heat to the surrounding areas."

She pauses for a moment, her head tilted as she studies the engine. Finally, she asks, "And what will power the fluid to move?"

He turns to smile at her. "I like your quick mind, Little Spark."

It's his first smile since she took him looking for the phoenix. She preens under his praise, straightening in her seat. She smiles back at him. "So, what's the answer?"

"There's an invention that's taking Lurin by storm in the northern region. A factory is using an engine to make its goods faster. They use something called gasoline to power it."

"Power it to do what?"

"Move more quickly. This one engine is taking the place of fifty men. I think that gasoline will work for my engine, too."

"It's like magic," Elora breathes, looking over the whole flying machine. "Can you imagine it actually in the air, flying by itself?" She smiles wide, closing her eyes to see it in her mind.

When she opens them, Duke is looking at her with a strange look. Then his face clears and he studies the engine. "Yes, I, uh, can imagine it very well. It's what keeps me motivated."

"Well, put me to work, dear Prince. I would very much like to work off my debt to you."

"Debt?" he gives her a small smile. "I thought I was the one who owed you. And it's more of an extortion, is it not?"

She flushes and looks away, picking up a tool and examining it closely. "Yes, well, call it what you want. I'm still willing to do anything to help this bargain along."

He glances at his hand and says, "Yes, that will be fulfilled. I have a month, don't I?"

"Yes, of course." She looks down, suddenly remembering how well her mother is already doing. "About that. I want to thank you for what you've already given me. It has helped greatly."

Studying her with his deep green gaze, he asks in a deep voice, "Truly? It has?"

She nods; her throat closed with emotion. She looks down at her lap to hide the moisture in her eyes.

"I'm glad," he says. "I'm doing all I can to help you. You know that don't you?"

He sounds so sincere she looks up, wiping a tear away quickly. She nods, her chest tightening. "You're responsible for my family's happiness."

So, the venom is for a woman in her family.

Duke agrees but looks uncomfortable with Elora's high praise. He nods. "Yes. Well, shall we begin?"

Elora wipes her face clear and nods, ready for anything. A burning desire to help the prince fills her to the point of bursting. "Absolutely."

Chapter Fourteen

The Prince

Working with Elora is so *easy*. She picks up on things so quickly. He moves fast through his tour. He thought he'd get stuck explaining things, but she seems to understand and even ask questions for elaboration. He's surprised to be enjoying himself more than ever.

She's a bright one, like I said.

He scoffs at Char, pausing in his description of a valve. 'When did you ever say she was bright?' he thinks.

I said she's perfect for you, so it's implied.

'You have no right to an opinion since you deliberately put yourself in harm's way tonight.'

I wanted to meet her myself. So, I did.

'I revealed that I knew your sex, Charlotte!'

"Uh, Prince." Elora eyes him with a strange expression, catching him in his inner monologue with Char. "You've already explained that the valve controls the amount of oil that enters the engine." Her eyes flit to the check valve he's still pointing at.

Blinking at her, he says, "Oh, I'm sorry, Little Spark."

She blushes. "It's alright, Prince."

"Please. Call me Duke."

Are you *blushing now, too? It's bad enough I have to see her doing it through your eyes, but I can tell when you're embarrassed. This romance is going to kill my sensibilities.*

'Char, I'm really going to wring your neck if you don't stop. It's not a romance. This is a business arrangement.' He grumbles inwardly at her.

She laughs so loudly, he winces at how it rings through his mind. *You keep telling yourself that. You're falling more and more in love with her as you go along, explaining your fascination with this tedious thing. And you love my neck too much to threaten it with violence.*

Duke holds in a sigh and returns his attention to Elora. "Yes, well, on to another subject. I'll have to create piping for the fluid to travel through."

Elora turns to him. "Will that be difficult, Pri—I mean, Duke?" She blows a piece of hair out of her eyes.

She distracts him by twisting a piece of her honey-gold hair around her finger. He's dying to know if it's as soft as it looks. He'd give anything to run his hands through it, then pull her to him ...

Duke stamps down that train of thought immediately. "Uh, yes, well, it will. I'd have to hire the blacksmith without telling him why I need it." He tears his eyes from her beautiful gaze. It seems he can't look at her without finding something else to admire. Her eyes are as distracting as her hair. Especially when they flash with intelligence. Why is she wasting her mind as a servant in the palace? "Although," he says, leaning back in his seat, "the easier thing to do would be to order it from the north where they have it in large supply for the factories."

She looks longingly into the distance at his mention of the northern factories.

He finds himself asking, "What is that expression for? Have you ever been to the north?"

She huffs. "I wish. No," she sighs. "I would love to travel, but I don't think that's going to be my path in life."

He puts down his tool and turns to her fully. "Why not?"

She shrugs. "My family depends on me for the money I make at the palace to live. There's no chance I can just up and leave."

He frowns. He's become so accustomed to his advantages in life. He wonders how it would feel to be trapped in one place. Well, he knows the feeling well as he's stuck in his identity as a prince. But to never have any opportunity to see other places? That would be tragic. "I'm sorry," he says in a sincere voice.

"It's life, Prince. Now, should we continue with my lesson?"

Respecting her wish to change the subject, he answers, "No, that's all I'll explain for tonight. You must be overwhelmed with all this information."

Her eyes narrow. "Do I look like a bumbling idiot, Prince?"

His stomach lurches. "No, of course not. In fact, you're incredibly bright. I didn't mean to imply anything else."

"Then why should we stop? I find I quite enjoy learning about your machine here."

"But it's a lot of information to take in, is it not?" As his first pupil for this gargantuan project, he wants to make as much use of her time as possible. And that won't be accomplished if he throws too many facts at her.

"Well, yes ..."

"And I would like you to retain most of this knowledge, so before I overfill your mind with even more information, let's get to actual work. I'd like to get some of this finished tonight."

He hides a smile when she frowns but doesn't disagree with him.

He flexes his hands. "Now, these hands are much too large to do intricate work, so that's where you'll come in."

She leans in, her eyes bright with excitement.

He takes in the moment, reveling in sharing his project with someone other than Char. She doesn't care one bit about his fascination with his machine.

I care very much. We'll fly together. If *you ever finish.*

'Well, then let me work, why don't you?'

Duke hands Elora a small screwdriver. "If you would be so kind, would you take these small screws here," he points at them on the table, "and help me get this piece screwed in?"

Her eyes widen. "I've never used a screwdriver before."

He smiles softly at her. "If you apply yourself here as well as you do baking, you'll do fine. Just turn it clockwise."

She nods, and when he places the iron piece he needs up to the machine, he holds it with one hand and points at the holes in it with the other.

Taking that as her cue, Elora picks up a small screw much easier than he could and fits it in one of the holes. Pressing the screwdriver to it, she turns the tool as instructed in slow, sure movements.

Her face, one of concentration before, now brightens like a light when she finishes. "I did it!"

He chuckles. "Of course you did. Now the next."

Sticking her tongue out in concentration, she repeats the procedure.

Duke can't help but watch her in stark appreciation. He's always respected a fine mind, but she's remarkably adept too. What could she accomplish given the chance? "Have you ever wanted to do anything else besides serving at the palace?"

"Baking," she says distractedly as her complete focus is on finishing attaching the piece he's holding.

"Besides baking," he says. Since her attention is on what she's doing, he can study her face without being noticed. Her small nose fits her face perfectly, and he can't decide what he appreciates more, her rosy cheeks or her fine pink lips.

She turns to him suddenly, catching him watching her.

He doesn't look away. He physically can't tear his gaze away from hers.

Her face deepens into a dark blush. "What...what are you looking at, Prince?"

"You. Your eyes are the color of molten gold. They're beautiful."

Her eyes sparkle even more against her blushing face. She looks down at her lap. The moment charges even more in a sort of expectancy when she looks up under her lashes. Her eyes are laced with interest.

Careful, Pet. Only make a move if you intend to do something about it later.

Char's words are like a douse of water on him, and he rears back, breaking eye contact. "Yes, well, let's continue. There's quite a bit more to do."

They continue in silence, but the air isn't uncomfortable with the moment they just shared. It feels more like a companionship, which is so strange to feel with a female. As Duke works, he compares his male friendships with this budding one and finds them similar, and yet different. There's a warmth with Elora he's never felt with anyone else before. He rather likes it.

As they move on to other pieces, he says, "I was hoping for some more of your baking tonight."

Elora immediately straightens. "Oh, I'm sorry, Pri—Duke. I had such a wonderful evening with my mother, since she's so much better, I completely forgot. It won't happen again. I promised you all kinds of delights, and I won't back out of our agreement."

"Elora, it's totally fine. I was just making conversation. But … your mother was unwell?" Now he's getting to the crux of why this little maid would dare blackmail the prince of the land.

Elora stiffens. Her eyes dart from his to the floor in quick movements. "Uh, she's just been a little under the weather lately." She bites her lip … again. He wishes she would stop doing that. The injustice of her poor lip suffering for her thoughts is almost unbearable.

But then his mind clears. It's suddenly obvious why she so desperately wants to hide her mother's illness. And why she needed the one medicine that can heal it. His heart drops. This can mean only one thing.

The wasting illness.

Char's right. He almost can't breathe. If word got out that Elora's mother has it, the entire family would be banished from all fae lands. He looks away, hiding his panic well. He's gotten very good at masking his true emotions.

'What am I going to do, Char?' he thinks frantically.

Find her the venom. Quickly. It can cure her mother.

Clenching his fist, he vows to do it. He's going to put pressure on his brother to come up with the venom he said he could get.

How he found himself depending on his kid brother is beyond him. But if he has to, he'll haunt his brother's steps continually.

Elora's existence here and her mother's life depend on it.

Chapter Fifteen

The Maid

As Elora walks home, her heart pounds from the prince's question about her mother. He had been quiet after she had given him a complete untruth. Did he suspect her mother has the wasting illness? She tries not to overthink the reasons for his silence.

He could have been concentrating, right? Of course, that's all it was.

She makes it home and falls into bed, her mind racing. Did she reveal too much? Does he suspect they have the wasting illness in their home? When the predawn light strikes the windows, she drifts to sleep.

Waking up to her father's booming laugh is like a balm to her soul. She jerks up and holds her foggy head. Blinking to get the cobwebs out of her mind, she takes a moment to wake up. But when she continues to hear her parents' voices, her mind clears like magic, and she bounds out of bed. She tugs her wrap on, slips on her mask and steps lightly out of her room and into her parent's room.

Her mother sits up in her bed, with a bowl of soup in her hands. She smiles warmly at Elora. "Hello, dear, how are you this morning?"

"Me?" she squeaks. "How are *you*, dear Mother?"

Mother looks from Father back to Elora, her face a little lost. "I'm feeling better, thank you. Not quite up to my usual self, but better. Well enough that I want to hear all that has gone on with you this past ... well, month that I've been ill."

Elora only too happily settles herself on the seat her father offers. She proceeds to tell Mother all that's gone on this past month, mentioning Candy, the other servants, her baking experiments. Everything except the prince.

When she looks out the window at the placement of the sun, she jumps up. "Oh, Mother, I have to go to work! I wish I could stay longer, but I'll return around two to check on you, then I'll be home for good at seven tonight."

Her mother nods and her father says, "I, too, have to go, my dear wife. I'm sorry to leave you. Are you all settled?"

"Yes, I'm comfortable. I have my books." She pats a stack of books that rests with her on the bed. Her father must have placed them there before Elora got up. "You two go and don't worry about me."

Elora steps from the house, a small smile on her lips, her heart elated at her mother's recovered energy. She knows it's short-lived; her mother needs the full dose of vampire venom to fully recover, but it energizes Elora, nevertheless.

The walk to the royal kitchens is just as pleasant as the start of her day. The sun is shining, everyone she passes waves hello, and the treehouses are all more beautiful than she remembered.

When she arrives in the kitchens, she's tying on her apron when Candy ambushes her.

"Why have you switched our shifts? What is going on, Elora? I know something is different with you. You're hiding something. Spill it. Whatever it is, I won't judge you."

Elora raises her eyebrows. "Judge what? The fact that I like to sleep in now instead of taking the morning shift?" Not even Candy is going to dim her joy.

"That," Candy says, pointing at Elora's face. "You're glowing. Why is that?"

"Girls!" Paula barks. "I expect the ballroom to be in perfect condition. I know Grant caught both of you dilly dallying the other day. None of that now."

"Yes, ma'am," they say in unison.

They walk toward the staircase, starting the massive climb up to the top.

Candy grumbles, "Why does Paula care about the state of the ballroom, anyway? Her domain is the kitchen."

Elora laughs. "Her domain is anywhere her food touches. She takes great pride in the presentation of her meals."

Candy shrugs and then leans in as a servant passes them on the stairs, "Let's get back to a much more delicious topic. Why are you glowing?"

"I'm not glowing, I'm just in a good mood. Ever had one of those?"

Candy lowers her voice further. "Is your mother recovered? Is that what this is about? You would have told me if she were, so I really don't think it's that."

Elora smiles. "My mother is doing better, in fact. You've hit the nail on the head."

Candy rears back, stopping her ascent. "I just said I don't think it's that. But Elora, that is wonderful news." She puts her hand on Elora's arm when they continue to trudge upstairs. Then her face brightens, her smile wide. "Wait, a minute. Maybe that look on your face is that you've been talking to someone. Who is it? Is it anyone I know?"

At Elora's wide-eyed expression, Candy jumps. "Oh, that is it. Hmm, who could it be? Michael the blacksmith? Justin the stablemaster's son? Oh, I know, Nicholas the Captain's son. But," she says, frowning. "when could you have talked to one of them?" She shakes her head and peers intently at Elora.

Elora keeps her face smooth of any emotion.

As they continue their ascent, Candy continues to muse. "The only males you've seen are the servants around here and of course, the princes," she finishes in a dismissive way, waving her hand. "But," she snorts. "None of the male servants are anyone you'd look twice at. It wouldn't be one of them. The only attractive males in this palace are the princes."

Elora thinks her face still resembles a blank expression, but Candy rounds on her and puts both hands on Elora's shoulders. "Elora Wincham, are you *talking* with one of the princes? Which one? It couldn't be the Prince Heir."

Elora winces.

Candy squeals. "It's *him*, isn't it? You're speaking with the Crown Prince. Oh, please. I *swear* you can hold me to secrecy for life. I'll even make a bargain if you promise to tell me details."

Elora turns to her friend, trying to corral her friend's wild questions. Her arm burns in warning. "Candy dear, don't offer bargains lightly. They are terrifyingly permanent. I would never put you in that position." Guilt blooms that she forced the prince to do one with her, but she'll choose not to think of that right now.

"I just mean it to that degree. *Please*, Elora, I'm dying to know." She leans into Elora's face.

Elora laughs lightly, wanting to tell her friend, but not even a new bargain would get her to do so. Her bargain with the prince would burn through her wrist and hand, slicing right through them, if she said one word about what the prince is doing. And she doesn't dare reveal that she's even meeting him at night. She's just going to have to let Candy think what she wants.

"It's really nothing, my friend, except my mother feeling better. Your imagination is getting away from you again."

Candy sniffs, then turns her steps up the stairs into a shuffle. "I was really hoping you had a tryst going with the Prince."

"Well, I'm sorry to disappoint you. I am having no tryst. With anyone." That much is true. Her time with the prince is solely a work arrangement. And blackmail.

Her mind turns to when she caught him looking at her last night. There was a certain admiration in his gaze. But surely that's not right. Maybe it's that her hair is quite unusual for this region. She owes her unique tresses and eye color to her mother's heritage. But, that moment in the workshop felt charged, like his admiration had shifted ...into something more.

"Are you two going to get started sometime today?" Grant barks at them from the landing to the royal rooms.

Candy jumps and squeaks in fright. "I'm so sorry, sir, we'll get going right away!"

"This is the third time I've had to talk to you, Elora. Don't make this a habit."

Chastised, Elora nods and joins Candy, who trembles in the royal hallway. She gives the elderly manservant an apologetic smile before she and Candy rush off to the supply room.

They grab buckets and rags and hurry to the ballroom to begin their work.

Elora walks in and takes a moment to look around the grand space with critical eyes. The three chandeliers need their crystals cleaned. And the eight wooden pillars need the paint touched up. Dusting the alcoves and polishing the king's and queen's thrones are also on the list. And of course, the floors. That's her first job. It needs a thorough cleaning. After they're all done, she'll go back over them.

Walking into the center of the cavernous place, she wonders what it would be like to be a guest and not the one cleaning. She takes her mop over to the bucket of water. After soaking and wringing it out, she glides the mop around, imagining Duke asking her to dance the opening waltz. Swirling, she can picture the prince leading her around the room. She closes her eyes, following the steps of the waltz, cradling the mop handle like a dance partner.

All reality flees with her imagination. Her muscles ache, not from hard work, but from dancing all night long. The past three nights were not to save her mother's life. They were nights of flirtation with the fae prince. He's captivated her with his true nature; one he reveals to her alone. Duke leads her in dances she'd begged her mother teach her.

She glides across the room. In a moment of whimsy, she switches her steps to a more quicker fae courtly dance, the Luriel.

Elora's eyes fly open when a hand comes around her waist and leads her in the actual steps. *Is she dreaming with her eyes open?*

"Am I better than a mop, Little Spark?" Duke asks in her ear. He pulls the mop away from her and tosses it across the room.

At the clattering noise, her dream vanishes, and she finds herself being led around the room by the man who, a moment before, starred in her daydreams.

"Personally, I would have chosen the waltz as our first dance, but the Luriel will do," Duke murmurs with a smile in his voice.

"What are you doing? We can't dance together!" Elora stiffens in his arms. But she can't help but follow his lead during the fast-paced dance.

"This is a ballroom, is it not?"

"What will the other servants say?" She looks around, but they're alone.

"I sent them away. I didn't think you'd want an audience." He continues to move in steps he was born to take. "Now, I much prefer the waltz." Expertly, he maneuvers her through the new steps and she follows his lead, speechless.

"I don't think this is appropriate," she says, fighting to keep her feelings from flying away from her.

He pulls her closer. "We are doing nothing I wouldn't do in front of hundreds of other people."

"But you're a..."

"Prince."

"And I'm a..."

"Beautiful woman enjoying a dance."

She blows out a breath. "That's not what I was going to say."

"And yet, you can't argue with facts."

She breaks his enigmatic gaze, looking down. Why not? There's no one watching. So, for one wild moment, she allows herself to make this memory. It will never happen again. She'll enjoy this dance with the fae prince. Relaxing in his arms, she breathlessly asks, "What made you come in here?"

He chuckles. "I was passing the ballroom, and you pulled me in here with your alluring dance. Watching you twirl with a mop, I couldn't resist cutting in."

Her heart beats wildly in her chest. He twirls her, making her head spin. Laying it on his chest, she whispers, "I didn't intend to draw you in here. I was just imagining."

"And now you're not. Whose arms were holding you in that dream?" His arms stiffen as he waits for her answer.

She smiles and looks up at him. "That's only for me to know, Prince."

Pulling her slightly closer to him, he whispers in her ear, "I was hoping you'd say it was me. I wish I could actually dance with you on the night of the ball."

At his words, reality crashes in, and Elora pulls away. She's a maid. He's a prince. They shouldn't be having this dance. Taking two full steps back, she looks up at him, a little out of breath. "But that could never happen, my Prince. Now, if you'll excuse me, I have duties to attend to."

With wooden steps, she walks across the room to retrieve her mop.

"Elora," Duke says, catching up to her, reaching for her wrist. "What's wrong?"

She pulls her arm out of reach, cradling it to her chest. In a tight voice, she says, "You know very well that this will be the only dance we'll ever have. I'm not meant for your world, Prince. I belong in the dark where I can be hidden."

"That's not …"

"It's the truth," she whips out and turns. "I'll meet you tonight, as your assistant. But that's all I'll ever be to you—the help."

"Elora," he says in a tone that brooks no argument. "You're wrong."

She spins to face him. "I've never been more correct, and you know it. Now, please leave." She points to the door. Even knowing she's commanding a prince in his own castle doesn't make her put her arm down. She stands her ground. Someone needs a good dose of reality.

He looks stunned at being dismissed, but with one look at her stony face, he nods and strides from the room.

Holding her middle to keep from unravelling completely, she takes measured breaths to contain the tears caused by her unvarnished reality. She could never be part of the prince's world. And as soon as she truly accepts that, her fragile peace will return.

Chapter Sixteen

The Prince

The dance with Elora fills his thoughts all day. But instead of taking time to ponder the event and her reactions: enjoyment and fury, he has to deal with two wearisome social engagements.

He has a private dinner with the Strafford family, who wants to stay for *hours,* and then suffers through a long night of poker. He's frustrated his mother continues to push the Strafford sisters at him and that his brother still hasn't produced the venom. Although he's promising it soon. And with a ball on the horizon, the sisters were full of gossip about attending nobles and hinting strongly for him to sign their dance cards.

The only dance card he wants to sign, however, will never exist: Elora's. Duke can't help but remember how perfectly she fits in his arms. He sighs when he realizes he'll only dance with women he has absolutely no interest in. He hangs his head in defeat. Duke breathes a quiet sigh of relief when he finally enters his hideaway workspace.

Char waits in the dark for him to light the lamps. *Your mother is really parading those sisters around to you, isn't she?*

He raises his tired gaze up to Char, taking in her graceful perch on one of the iron seats he hung around the room. Her long tail feathers drape over the side in a cascade of crimson and dark amber. There's not a flicker of fire in sight tonight, so she must be in a good mood.

"I know I have to choose a wife, but I can't bring myself to care in that way for either of the Strafford sisters." He massages his stiff neck muscles. Immediately his mind flies to twirling around a smiling Elora.

If you hadn't met a certain someone, you might have tolerated Lady Elizabeth well enough.

"Stop it, Char. I mean it."

You have choices now; that's all I'm saying. And you know who I mean.

"Char," he sighs and runs a hand over his eyes. "Please just drop it. And it's time you left. Elora will be here any moment."

I am not leaving.

Duke snaps his head up. "What did you say?"

You heard me.

"Char, you can't be seen ... again. If Elora sees you here—"

She'll what? Tell the King she saw a phoenix? She hasn't yet. She's seen me twice now. And she would never. Besides, she thinks I'm beautiful.

Clenching his fists, he stalks over to her. "That was before. She can't know that we're mind-melded!"

Calm down, Prince. It would make no difference to her. It would intrigue her. I'm telling you, the two of you have a connection. It's time I'm a part of that.

Fuming, he stares at his pet. When she stares back at him defiantly, he warns, "I will make you leave."

Ha! How?

In answer, he jumps, lunging for her. She squawks, rearing back, avoiding his grasp. Her tail flares up in flames. He ignores them and lunges again. He swipes at her, one hand passing through the flames, but thanks to his elemental gifting it doesn't harm him. But she dodges and flies across the room.

You're acting like a child. I'm warning you. Leave me alone.

Racing after her, he jumps to reach her. Again, she flies up, her body fully on fire this time.

Last chance. I'm warning you, Prince.

When he swipes at her, she retaliates, clawing him. Her strike does its job, and he hisses, leaning down over his now-bleeding hand.

"Confound it, Char, you cut me!" Blood flows freely from four long cuts on the top of his hand. There are of course, no burns as he's impervious to flames. He reaches for a cloth and wraps it around his hand. "Why did you do that?" Pain flares, and he holds his hand to his chest.

She peers at him imperiously. *I would think that is obvious. I warned you.* She banks her fire, but the ends of her tail feathers still flame with her agitation.

Duke's shoulders slouch in defeat. "I really don't think this is a good idea."

Have more faith in the girl.

It's at that moment that the door opens. "Duke? Who are you talking to?" Elora steps in with hesitating steps. She's holding a plate with what looks like baked goods on it. When she sees Char in the back of the room, she gasps loudly, covering her mouth with her hand, fumbling with her plate. She manages to hold on to it. "It's you! Oh!" Her wide eyes travel over Char and her burning tail. "She's on fire," she says in awe, turning to Duke.

"I am aware," he growls, hiding his bleeding hand.

"What is she doing here?" She freezes in her tracks, returning her gaze back to Char, who watches her back with interest.

"I have no idea." At those words, Char squawks and jumps in her seat, spreading fiery wings all around her in a golden, showy display.

Don't make me burn your little pet project to the ground.

"Okay, okay," he concedes, holding up his uninjured hand. "I'll tell her the truth. Just calm down." He glances at his flying machine with concern.

Start talking soon, or I make no promises.

Blowing out a breath, he turns to Elora, whose golden eyes have gotten impossibly wider.

She glances between him and his burning pet.

"Douse those flames, and I'll tell her," he growls at Char.

Char complies, and smoke billows when she puts out her tantrum.

"Duke?" Elora whispers.

"Char is my pet," he grudgingly says. "She can communicate with me telepathically."

Char chirrups with pleasure at his words.

"Oh," Elora breathes. "Truly? That's wonderful. You're mind-melded with her?" she squeaks. "What a gift!" Elora takes a step towards her. "So, she understands me too?"

"Of course."

"Oh, my." Then she blushes. "I'm sorry," she tells Char. "I must seem like a bumbling idiot, but I'd like to introduce myself."

Char turns fully toward her, cocking her head.

"My name is Elora Wincham. I'm a maid in the palace, and I'm helping the prince with his flying machine."

Char chirrups again, pleased to be spoken to. *I like her very much. Tell her I said so.*

Duke side-eyes her with annoyance but says to Elora, "She says she likes you very much."

Elora's mouth drops open. She blinks. "She does? After just that introduction?"

"Well," he says, walking over to his worktable, reaching for his stool with his good hand. He winces at the pain in his other hand, cradling it to his chest. He slumps down into his seat. "She has seen everything I have since I met you. So, you can say she has a good idea of who you are."

"She does? And she likes me?" Her eyes are wide and lovely.

He smiles. "Yes, she does."

Elora walks over to the table, setting down the plate. She clasps her hands together to her chest. "Well, I think you're pretty wonderful, too," she tells Char, beaming at her.

Char chirrups and flies closer to Elora. She trails her tail feathers, which are blessedly not on fire, on Elora's shoulder as she passes her, and Elora laughs in delight. Char settles herself on the seat that's closest to the worktable and looks down at the plate.

Is she going to give you her gift?

Duke looks down at the plate with interest. "What did you bring?"

"Oh! I made you chocolate croissants. It took me a couple of failed batches, but I finally got them right."

He looks at her, cocking his head. "You don't seem like you make mistakes easily. Not baking ones."

She flushes, looking down. "I was distracted tonight."

Immediately he wonders if their dance inspired her clumsiness. He hasn't been able to think of anything else all day. "By what?"

"I think you know," she finally answers, her blush deepening.

Ooooo, that blush is telling.

Duke glares at Char before he returns his gaze to Elora.

She watches him and Char with interest. "You two are talking, aren't you?" she asks.

"Yes. Isn't it obvious?" he asks curtly, suddenly frustrated he can't pursue things with Elora. He very much wants to.

You're very grouchy.

"Maybe I should go home," Elora says quietly. She starts to rise.

He holds out his injured hand. "I'm sorry, Elora. I don't know what's wrong with me. Forgive me for my bad mood."

She spies his injury. "What did you do to your hand?" She bends down to hold it.

He freezes at her touch.

"May I?" she asks, fingering the edges of the towel.

He nods, swallowing.

She peels the edges away and gasps when she sees the angry red slashes. She looks up sharply at Char. "Was this you?"

Char looks away almost disinterestedly.

"Did she *cut* you?" Elora's voice has a protective sound to it, directing her flashing eyes at him.

"Yes."

"Why?"

"We had a disagreement." He shrugs.

"About what?"

He looks up at her. "You," he says quietly.

"Me?" she asks with alarm. She looks over his cuts with concern and asks, "Do you have any astringent here?"

He nods his head towards the kit of medical supplies on the corner table.

She releases his hand, which makes him miss her soft touch. Walking over to the table, she grabs the kit and, holding it to her chest, says to Char, "I'm sorry, but that is no way to treat a friend," before she marches back to him.

He can only watch as she sits down next to him and starts caring for his injuries.

You're welcome.

Ignoring Char, he watches Elora as she cleans his wounds with gentle fingers and tsks.

"These really need stitches," she mutters.

He winces at the sting of the antiseptic. "No, I'll just keep it wrapped. They will heal."

Elora purses her lips but doesn't argue. "I'm sorry," she says quietly, "that I was the reason you two quarreled. You didn't want me to know about her?"

"No, I didn't."

"I will never say anything about her. To anyone. Besides her temper, she's magnificent. I wouldn't want to see a single feather harmed."

I told you.

He nods at Char.

"I wish I could hear her speak though," Elora says, finishing his dressing.

She can. If she marries you.

He looks up in alarm. He did *not* know that. 'Are you sure?' he thinks.

Very.

"What did she just say? I could see surprise on your face," Elora says, her face bright with curiosity.

"Nothing," he says firmly, getting up from his seat. "Come, let's get started. We're running late."

Elora is quiet for a moment, watching Char, who returns her gaze. Finally getting up, she follows Duke to the table with tools spread all over it. Nothing has changed since her last visit. "So, you haven't been here all night? You just got here, too?"

"Yes, it was, unfortunately, a late night for me."

"You were pretending to be bored and unmotivated?" she asks, almost in disapproval.

He glances at her with amusement. "It's the story of my life."

"It shouldn't be."

I really like this girl. She's absolutely right.

"Why can't people know you as you really are?" She accepts the tools he hands her and holds them to her chest. She follows him back to the worktable.

"Because princes have been lazy for centuries, as long as there's been a royal family."

"I have a hard time believing there wasn't one industrious fae prince in all the past centuries."

"None that have been recorded."

"Well, I think that is ridiculous. And you should feel that way too," she says in a sharp tone.

He cocks an eyebrow at her. "My opinion is hardly one that matters."

"But you're the *prince*," she cries. "You matter."

"Thank you."

She blows out a frustrated breath. "If I were you, I would change all those preconceived notions and ..." She trails off, leaving the sentence unfinished.

"What? What exactly would you do?"

She straightens. "I would work on my flying machine during the day and not care what anybody thinks."

He shifts to face her. "And when the nobles say you're wasting your very valuable time on a project that may or may not work?"

She sniffs. "You don't know that it won't work. And I would defend my project with my life."

He stares at her. "You don't think I want to do that?"

"Then *why*? Why don't you?"

Stifling frustration, he crosses his arms, trying to be patient with her. "I am to do one thing with my life. That is to rule this country. Once I'm king, I will be making decisions that will affect every single fae in Nebraria. Until then, I'm to act like a prince. Attend royal functions, establish relationships with the leading nobles, all in a parade of one social engagement after another. If my parents were to find out about this project, they would think I'm wasting my formative years on a distraction. I know that right now all it looks like I'm doing is one social event after another, but my parents have groomed me to use them to curry favor with the nobles for when I'm king."

She nods, but then her head swings to his. "Wait, a *distraction*?" She waves her hands at the machine. "This is marvelous. Imagine if you had a team of people helping you. You'd accomplish so much more than I ever could."

"Again, it would be time spent away from my true duties. Which is not acceptable. I've been trained from birth to follow the steps of every king before me. That will not change."

She presses her lips together like she wants to say something more but stays silent.

"I've resigned myself to my life. You need to, as well."

"The problem is, Duke, you don't know me very well."

Now that much is true, he thinks as he puts his tools all in order.

"Well, until I do, let's get to work," he says, shutting down any notion of changing the way things have been for thousands of years.

Chapter Seventeen

The Maid

E lora sits stiffly next to Duke, who keeps her busy with instructed tasks. Once there's a lull, she says with a huff, "Haven't you ever wanted to be bold?"

He turns from the engine, his deep green eyes studying her. "Yes."

"Well, were you?"

"Depends." He shrugs.

"On what?" She desperately wants him to realize his true worth. *Why is he so afraid to reveal his nature?*

"Sometimes I act on my feelings. Other times ..." His arresting eyes turn troubled, and he extends his hand for a tool.

She hands him the wrench he needs and asks, "Other times, what?"

He blows out a breath, leaning on the table, studying his work. As he attaches a bolt, he says, "It really depends on the situation, but generally I have no issue being a bold guy." He looks back at her with a smirk. His eyes darken as they flick to her lips and back to her eyes.

Her mouth dries at his implication. She leans back, folding her arms. "That's not what I meant."

"Oh, I know what you meant. And we've discussed this already." He finally releases her gaze and turns back to his work. "By the way, the pipes will be here soon, we'll put them in when they arrive."

She blows out a breath, rubbing her forehead. A yawn catches her by surprise. "These late nights are getting to me."

He looks at her with concern. "Why don't you take the next night off? With your work at the palace, you're going to run yourself ragged."

"No," she says firmly, straightening. "I can do this. I *need* to do this." She rearranges the screws on the table, from largest to smallest.

Duke leans back, putting his fist on his lap. "Elora, I know we have an agreement, but you won't be of any use to me if you're exhausted. Plus, you're baking for me." He shakes his head. "It's too much."

She smiles softly at him, appreciating his worry. "I'll see how I feel later. I traded a friend for the afternoon shifts this month, so I can sleep in. And I love baking, remember?"

His expression softens. "I remember and so enjoy your efforts." With that, he picks up his third croissant and eats it in three bites. "I'm going to get fat like my father if I continue eating like this."

"I doubt that." She giggles at the chocolate residue on the side of his mouth. Before she can think it through, she reaches over to wipe it off. She freezes, her hand cupping his face, with her thumb where the chocolate was. When she sees his expression, she realizes she's leaned quite close to him.

He turns his head a fraction and softly kisses her fingers. "Thank you," he says huskily.

Elora couldn't move even if she wanted to. His lips on her fingers immobilize her. Suddenly, she needs to know what his lips would feel like on hers. Her lips part when she realizes she's leaned in further. *When did she move?*

"Elora." Duke's voice sounds strangled. He seems to war with himself before he grabs her neck, pulling her in to meet his lips.

Duke frames her head in hands, pressing his lips against hers in a frantic, almost reverent way. Her blood heats up at his kiss, almost to a boiling point. She can't remember how this kiss started, only that she doesn't want it to end. She runs her hands through his silken wavy hair.

Almost as if she's reminded him of her own hair, he reaches behind her to untie the string holding her hair back. It releases her hair into a wild, wavy mess. He pulls away and threads his fingers through her strands, worshiping her with his eyes. He spreads her hair across her shoulders and inhales sharply. He leans in, frames her face again and kisses her lips in gentle touches, then her cheeks. He moves on to press feather-light kisses to her eyes then says, "I love your eyes. Elora, look at me."

She couldn't look anywhere else, so she easily complies. He looks at her with such intent she has to ask, "What are you thinking?"

"That I could do this all night," is his swift response. As if to prove his words true, he leans in and kisses her softly.

His gentleness sparks a fire in her only he can contain. She presses her lips more firmly to his and initiates a deeper kiss that makes him groan. She can taste the chocolate from her dessert, and it thrills her.

Tearing his lips away from hers, he presses his forehead to hers, breathing heavily. "Elora, give me a moment."

She nods, burying her face in his neck, inhaling his deep musk scent. Unable to help herself, she kisses his neck, tasting it, too.

Lunging back, he holds out his hands. "I need a moment. Please. I need to think."

Drunk on pleasure, she leans in to return to the wonderland that his kisses bring her to.

Jumping off his chair, Duke takes three steps away from her and paces. "This ... this changes things. We need to think this through."

Frustrated he ended a kiss so wonderful, she watches him pace. She knows she'll be dreaming about those kisses for days. Then the reality of their situation hits her. This was highly inappropriate to do, being unmarried.

Duke only hammers it in when he says, "As a prince, my ... attentions can be misconstrued easily."

"Misconstrued?" Her stomach twists.

Regret fills his expression. "I don't want to make a mistake with you, do things too fast."

"A *mistake*? Is that what that was?" Her heart hammers in her chest, and her eyes blind her with tears.

"No! You're not—that wasn't a mistake. I've been wanting to do that from the first moment you walked inside this bunker. I'm just trying to be careful ... with my heart and yours. Let's not do that again until we're sure where we're going to go with it." He gives her a tortured expression.

Elora nods miserably. It was just a kiss. Well, several kisses. Not a start to a relationship. They could never have a future together. Not as long as she's a maid in the palace and he's the prince. Tears spill onto her cheeks, and she wipes them away impatiently. "I understand," she says in a deadpan voice.

"Elora, please believe me. I would like nothing more than to continue."

"No, Prince. I understand. Let's resume working. The sooner we can finish this flying machine, and you give me my money, the sooner I can forget ... about all of this." Her stomach plunges at the thought of not working with Duke anymore, but she doesn't see any other way for them to continue their lives. They can never be together, so why torment themselves?

She glances up at him. His tortured expression only makes the ache in her stomach worse. But she hardens her resolve. "I trust you will have the money to fulfil the bargain soon?"

"I should have what you need in a few days, hopefully." He winces and glances at his arm.

"Okay. Shall we?" She gestures toward the machine, and he reluctantly sits down to resume work.

The night passes in uncomfortable silence. Elora wishes she'd never kissed the prince. But now that she has, she will have to mourn the loss of any future kisses. Those will never be.

Chapter Eighteen

The Prince

After his kiss with Elora, Duke hunts almost feverishly to find a way to properly court her. He comes up empty every time. She can't pass for a noble since her face is too recognizable in the palace as one of the chief maids. And that would be the only way that would satisfy his parents and the noble class.

He's never felt this way about any fae woman and knows he never will again. There must be a way for her to be part of his world. But after several sleepless nights, and what seems like weeks of mindless societal events, thinking it over, he's no closer to an answer.

Until he finds one, he must keep his distance. But he sorely misses the easy companionship they shared. She did not return to his bunker the night after their shared kiss, but she did the following evening. She was civil, but they seemed to agree not to discuss what happened between them.

As excruciating as it is, they work in a professional manner for a little over a week with the air tense between them. The pipes arrive, and they continue to build the engine, moving quickly until he finds that he's close to testing it out.

The morning of the day comes when he plans to try to start the engine. He resolves to find his brother and demand to know when he will have the venom. "Grant, do you know where my brother would be? I checked in the breakfast room, and he wasn't there."

Grant taps his leg. "I recall his manservant telling me the prince has taken a sudden interest in staff training again, sir. You might find him down on the training grounds."

Duke nods and changes his clothes to his fighting leathers. With all the pent-up angst he feels over Elora, it sounds like a perfect plan to blow off steam. He exits his room and as he's about to walk down the steps, his mother's voice calls out to him.

"A moment, Son?"

Fighting a grimace, he turns and forces a pained smile. Anxiety careens through him fighting for an escape. "Yes, Mother?"

She approaches him, fully dressed for the day in a deep red gown with elaborate green embellishments. "Invitations have gone out to all the noble families in the land for the Midnight Ball. I wanted to thank you for your idea. I do hope your intention was to finally decide on a bride. But regardless, now, it must be."

His mind immediately flies to Elora. He wholeheartedly wants to disagree with his mother but now is not the time. His heart races at her words and he suddenly has the cloying feeling like he can't breathe.

"I've already had the ballroom cleaned, and with a few minor adjustments, it will be ready. Grant is aware of my expectations."

His mind flies to his shared dance with Elora as she cleaned said ballroom. He forces himself to pay attention to his mother.

"Now," she says, raising her eyebrow at him, "From you, I require full cooperation. No more dragging your feet in selecting your future bride. And remember, she will be queen one day, so choose well. And, in case you don't choose one, I've selected the perfect woman for you."

His strangled throat croaks out, "Who?"

Mother's eyes light up. "It was difficult to choose, but I've settled on Lady Mary."

Suddenly, it feels like a full-grown dragon sits on his chest. Rubbing it, he mumbles, "Would you excuse me? I need to find Harry."

She nods, releasing him from their conversation, and he all but flies down the stairs to escape into the fresh air. Once he pushes through the heavy oaken door, he takes deep inhales, trying to loosen the tightness in his chest. *Creator, help! I know my place but help me choose the right wife. Make Elora a possibility. I cannot possibly marry Lady Mary Strafford.*

With that prayer in mind, he breathes in the cool, fresh air as he tries to clear his head. He walks briskly to the training grounds in search of his brother. Before he reaches it, the sound of clacking fills the air. Walking up to the yard, he sees quite a good group assembled, with twenty pairs of soldiers dominating the space all fighting with their traditional fighting weapon, the staff. That suits him fine.

His body is primed for a good fight, and if one won't do, several will. His brother is currently in a match, so Duke walks to the fence. He jumps over it, too impatient to walk over and open the gate. Giving his brother time to finish, Duke strides over to the staffs and finds his waiting for him in the same place he left it last time. No one would dare use his personal weapon. He grips it, holding it out to appreciate its perfect balance. The woodworker who crafted it did so with his preferred wood, red oak. Its strength under duress complements his fighting style, which favors hard strikes. He smooths his hand over the red grain pattern, appreciating the dents and imperfections showcasing his past matches.

Harry approaches, having finished his bout. He's out of breath and carrying his rattan wood weapon. Duke smirks. Harry needs the lightweight wood since he's not yet as strong a fighter as Duke or the other fae soldiers.

Harry guesses Duke's thoughts and twirls his weapon above his head, bringing it down to lean on. "Don't knock my staff; I'm practically a beginner."

Duke huffs a laugh. "You wouldn't be if you had attended our lessons when we were younger."

Harry blows his dark hair out of his face. "I had better things to do with my time."

"I can see that. You've always chased down whatever strikes your fancy, and that's usually young women. Speaking of," Duke leans in and asks in a low voice, "has your vampire *lady friend* come up with the venom yet?"

Harry eyes him with a smile. "How did you know it was a woman?"

Duke chuckles. "Because with you it always is, Brother."

"You might be right about that, but there are a lot of things you don't know about me, Duke. Like you, I keep secrets."

Duke bristles. "What do you mean?"

Harry smirks at him knowingly. "Let's just say I know you favor nocturnal activities."

Duke stiffens. "How about we cut the talk and have a bout?

Harry twirls his staff and backs up in answer, holding his arms open wide. "Be happy to."

Duke takes no time to swing down hard on his brother's weapon, before swiftly bringing his own back up to hit Harry's chin. He uses wind to give his staff more speed.

Harry narrowly dodges and raises his staff back up in a defensive stance. He shoots out a bright orange fireball. Duke steps back and smacks it away with one hard swing.

Duke calls out, "So, we're playing with fire today? Don't you usually favor water?"

Harry grins as he blocks Duke's next two hits. "I have to keep you on your toes."

Both fall silent as they focus on their match, loud clacks filling the air for several minutes. In a valiant effort to keep up, Harry steps back. A six-foot ice spear quickly forms to a deadly point. Lunging back, he throws it at Duke. Duke throws up a firewall, melting the ice weapon and laughs. "So, you do resort to using water."

"I have to use what talents I have to attempt to beat you."

"Well, that's not going to be today." Duke tires of playing with his younger brother. Using a blast of wind to speed up his staff, he sweeps Harry's feet sending him crashing to the ground, landing on his back.

Harry lies still for a moment, breathing hard and blinking up at the sky. "I need to learn how you do that."

Duke puts his hand out to help his brother up. "You watch your opponent's feet."

With a groan, Harry stands up, rubbing the back of his head. "I'm too busy watching what your staff is doing to bother worrying about your feet."

Duke gives a short laugh. "That's why you end up on your back every time."

"Sorry I couldn't help, Brother."

Duke ignores him and turns toward an evenly-matched fight. It's the blacksmith's son and a soldier. He frowns at the pair. *Why is it that either one of these men can court Elora and he can't?* The two finish when Michael, the son of the blacksmith, spins and confuses the soldier with a faux hit, then shoves the soldier down, holding his staff above the soldier's throat.

Duke claps and walks up to Michael. "Care for a match with me?"

If Michael is surprised the prince heir requests a match with him, he hides it very well. He nods and gets into position. Duke's blood roars in anticipation of a good fight. His opponent is large, spinning his weapon lazily with one hand. Duke wonders which elemental gifts he will use.

Michael doesn't wait before sweeping his staff over his head and bringing it down low, aiming for Duke's knee. Duke knocks it away and then spins. He swings at the man's middle and lands a hit.

"Oomph," Michael grunts and wheezes a breath, bending over. He clambers backward, protecting his middle.

Duke advances, but Michael recovers well enough to rush up a long brown root in an explosion of dirt. Covering his eyes so he's not blinded, Duke stumbles when the root tangles his legs. Duke has to be swift and burn them off quickly. Using wind, he swings down hard, meeting Michael's staff. *Why can't I have this man's life?* Michael knocks Duke's strike away and then, with his mind, sends a flurry of broken tree branches at Duke, all aiming to impale him.

Duke sweeps his arm, using wind to blow them away. He lunges back when some come through, slicing his arm and leg. Shaking off the sharp stings, Duke blocks a hit meant to clip him under his chin. *Does this man know how lucky he is?* Duke spins and swings down aiming for the man's arm, a strike that could break it. *Elora could be mine if I had this blacksmith's life.* Michael's face registers surprise as he knocks away the blow.

Michael jumps toward him, aiming for Duke's head and shoulders. Even though Duke shifts his body, he can't smack all the blows away, one lands hard on his right shoulder. Ignoring the pain of the strike, he aims for Michael's middle, trying to keep the man's aim lower.

By this time, the other fights have stopped, and a circle of men surrounds the prince and his opponent. Aware of them, Duke ignores the audience and concentrates on his match.

Both are sweating when Michael, in a burst of speed, sends a flurry of hits combined with two roots to tangle Duke's feet. Avoiding both the strikes and the roots makes Duke stumble and his right-hand grip loosens. He has to tighten his hold on his left hand, so the man won't knock the weapon away completely. Duke plants his feet, burns the roots away then retreats to give himself a moment to regroup. Michael advances. Duke's mind runs. *Why?* He blasts Michael with one hard strike after another, alternating between striking his head and his middle. *Why can't the Creator give me the one thing I want?* He won't allow any more mistakes. *Why must I fight for everything?*

Michael stumbles as Duke advances. He ignores the pain from the strikes he's suffered and tries to sweep Michael's feet out. Unlike Harry, Michael anticipates the move and jumps to avoid tripping.

"Is that all you've got, Crown Prince?" Michael taunts.

Duke eyes him hard. *All I want is to lay claim to a heart that can never be mine. If this man wanted, Elora could easily be his.* Fury roars through him at the thought. He jumps and twirls his staff above his head to gain momentum, not even needing wind to aid him and swings down hard on Michael's staff, knocking it from his grasp. Stumbling, Michael falls to the ground.

Breathing hard, Duke stares down at the blacksmith's son who watches him warily. Duke advances two steps to shake his hand, but Michael flinches. When Duke moves the staff to his left hand, Michael cowers, holding both arms above his head. Duke freezes. *Does he think I will strike him while he's defenseless?* Bowing his head, he's ashamed he took his frustrations out on an innocent man.

"Brother?" Harry puts his hand on Duke's stiff shoulder, pulling him away. "What's wrong?" he asks quietly.

"Nothing," Duke says, panting.

"That wasn't nothing."

Duke looks around and realizes the men are all rumbling, wondering what his problem is.

Duke grimaces and says to Michael, "Nice fight." He doesn't move, only holds out his hand.

Wiping his forehead with his sleeve, Michael gets back to his feet and takes a cautious step, taking Duke's hand, shaking it hard. "Thank you, Prince. It was an honor. Is all well?"

With those words, all the fight leaves Duke. "Yes, I just needed to let off some steam."

Michael nods like he understands and Duke turns away, walking over to the wall of staffs, putting his away.

Harry follows him. "How does an ale sound?"

"Sounds like two would be better," he answers with a grim smile.

He and Harry walk to the nearest tavern. They're both quiet on the way there. When they enter the tavern and the owner sees who they are, they are quickly welcomed and given a clean table.

Duke flops down in his seat, blowing out a breath and putting his head in his hands.

"So, are you going to tell me what that fight was really about?" Harry asks. He thanks the owner when he puts two brimming mugs of ale before them.

With only Char to truly talk to about his secret life, Duke sorely wants to unburden to another fae, even if it's his brother. But when he looks at Harry, he expects to find amusement in his gaze, but there's only concern.

"I know you've been secreting yourself away most nights for the past year at least," Harry says, leaning his elbow on the table so he can talk low. "And I have no idea what you're doing, but I'd like to help you, if I can."

Duke blows out a slow breath and wonders how Harry knows that much. "I don't know where to start," he finally says.

"How about at the beginning?"

"Can I trust you not to tell anyone?" Duke asks.

"I've kept your secret all this time, haven't I?"

Duke nods slowly. So, in a low tone, he tells his brother everything. His flying machine, Char, Elora, their mother's demand he finds a bride, everything. Harry listens, reacting with quiet surprise at each pivotal moment, but allowing Duke to finish without once interrupting him. He just drinks his ale as he listens. Once Duke completes his long tale, a huge weight comes off his chest.

Harry leans back in his seat, smooths his hand over his mouth and looks at Duke as if in a new light. He laughs softly. "I admit, I did not expect all of that. You have quite a situation on your hands. Are you truly building, with Elora's help, a machine that will fly?"

Duke nods.

Waving in the air, Harry asks, "Forget that question, I can't get my mind around it. Which facet of all this is the most pressing?"

Duke answers quickly. "Elora. Help me get her to the ball. I want to choose her as my queen."

Harry's eyebrows shoot up. "You're that certain she's the one?"

Duke gives two hard nods. "I am."

Harry thinks for a moment then nods. "You've just given me an especially fun pet project. I will be like her fairy godfather, transforming your maid into someone fit to be queen. Let me handle everything. But first, we need to make the ball a masquerade. Again, leave that in my hands. I'll talk to Mother, and we'll get the notice out through the couriers to the nobles. We'll need to cover your girl's pretty face if we're going to make this work."

Duke nods, hope soaring through his chest. "If I choose her as my bride with her behind a mask, what happens when we unveil her?"

Harry looks uneasy. "I haven't figured that part out yet. Let me think on that."

Duke nods. He puts his hand on his brother's shoulder. "I couldn't do this without you, Harry. Thank you."

Harry chuckles. "Thank me when this is all over. Oh, and I'll get the venom to our little princess too. I'm working on it."

Duke breathes easier knowing Elora's mother will get the medicine she needs. That will make all the difference in the world to Elora if she's to be convinced to attend the ball. "And just how do you plan on approaching Elora about all of this?"

"Oh, no. You're not getting all of my secrets with the ladies out of me. I'll handle it, okay?"

Duke bristles at the thought of what Harry's implying. "She's mine, don't forget that."

"Believe me, I know. Don't worry, Brother, I'll handle her with brotherly gloves."

Duke nods, satisfied, and they finish their ales. Duke leaves to return to his blasted social duties at the palace.

Chapter Nineteen

The Prince

Char had been sleeping during the day, so that night in the bunker, Duke relates the discussion with his brother to her.

Why can't you just announce her as your bride? Why go through all this nonsense? Hiding her behind a mask? Ridiculous.

Duke sighs. "How many times must I tell you that I can't just do what I want? I have my mother, father, and the nobles to think about."

What is the point of being heir to the kingdom when you have no real power?

"I do have power. It just needs to be carefully managed."

And you trust your brother to take care of all this?

The doubt in her voice echoes how he used to view his brother, but Harry has surprised him. He's getting his hands on the costly, elusive venom Elora needs. If he can do that, he can handle getting Elora to the ball. Hopefully.

Just wait. Elora will surprise you all. She has an indefinable element in her character that will defy all preconceived notions.

"I know. I've seen it myself."

Elora knocks softly on the door, as she's done the past several nights. He winces because she's become quite formal lately.

His heart clenches as she enters. It's drizzling outside, so her head is covered with her cloak when he answers the door. She moves to take it off, but it unravels her hair tie and loosens her hair. It falls in waves around her. That sight always makes his heart race.

She seems embarrassed at her appearance, because as soon as she lays the cloak down, she immediately reaches to pick up the ribbon. She tries to tie her hair back, but her fingers fumble, trying several times to knot it. Her fingers must be cold.

Giving up on watching her struggle, Duke gets up and steps behind her, saying quietly, "Here, allow me." When he reaches for the ribbon, his fingers brush against hers and a static electricity flies between them.

"Sorry, Little Spark. You're living up to your name."

"Don't call me Little Spark," she says quietly.

His heart falls with her words, and he stands mutely behind her. He inhales, and her soft sweet scent fills his senses, quickening his breath. She must have been baking. But he doesn't see her creations. That proves she's upset with him. He ties the ribbon around her hair while she stands still. As much as he would like to draw out the moment, she's so stiff, he forces himself to step back.

"How are you?" he asks quietly, very aware that she's still turned away.

"Fine." When she turns, pain flashes in her eyes as she glances at him and then away just as quickly.

He flinches at her words. He would do just about anything to recover their lost easy friendship.

I told you to be careful of your actions, Duke. Now look what your clumsy attempt at romance has done to our poor Elora. She's not herself.

Ignoring Char, he jumps to the thing he thinks will make her happiest. He says, "I think I'm ready to test out the engine tonight. And I was thinking that maybe I could teach you how to fly the machine."

His offer seems to jerk her out of her somber mood. Her eyes widen, and she puts her hand on her chest. "You want to teach *me* how to fly this?" She looks over his machine with quiet awe.

Happy he's managed to pull her out of her shell, he answers quickly. "Yes, of course. I'll have to make some modifications so you can reach the pedals, but I'd be happy to teach you."

Her pretty face scrunches in thought before her look brightens. "I could fly? Truly?"

Duke gives a short laugh. He runs his hand through his hair. "Well, that's if it works. I'd have to teach myself first and take many, many test flights to be sure it's safe enough, but, yes."

She studies the engine with a new kind of fascination. "Well, let's see if it even turns on. That's the first step, yes?" Then her forehead furrows. She looks around the room. "I see you've built yourself a grand machine, but how are you planning to get it out of the underground bunker?"

His heart soars. Now they're having a productive conversation. He rubs his hands together. "Well, that's where my dear Char will help me."

Elora looks at Char with a sheepish expression. "I'm sorry, Char, dear, I haven't said hello to you yet. Forgive me."

Char chirrups in response but chastises Duke in the same breath, *See? She's uncomfortable. You did that.*

Without looking over at his pet, he thinks back, 'I didn't plan that. And she's more herself now. Leave me be.'

Elora looks between him and Char, seeming to sense they're speaking mind to mind.

"You see," Duke says, "Char amplifies my gift with our bond. Using my earth and wind elements, and with Char funneling me with her energy, I'm going to make a tunnel. Then the flying machine can roll out on its wheels."

"Huh," Elora says. Then she rolls up her sleeves. "So, how does it work? How will you fly this thing?"

He chuckles. "I'll give you my theory, because without testing it out, that's all it is, and I have to be sure the engine will even turn on." When she nods, he turns and gestures for her to come to his side next to the pilot seat. "First thing is when you sit, you pull this cord hard and, hopefully, the engine will turn on." He points to a cord in front of the seat. "Then, you slowly pull the throttle, this," he points at a short handle on the dashboard. "It's going to make the propellers spin faster and faster the more you pull the handle. It will move the craft forward until you gather speed, and it's my theory that it's the speed that will make you take flight. Now," he points at the pedals on the floor. "Those are like the rudders of a ship. They will adjust the yaw, the ability to turn left and right in the tail. And it will make you fly straight." Then he directs her attention to the long handle coming out of the floorboards. "This is the control stick. It will allow you to turn the plane in whatever direction you choose."

Elora listens attentively as she leans over the side, looking over all the elements he explained. She turns to him. "Are you excited or scared to test this out?"

He grins. "Ecstatic. I can't wait to see if all my wild ideas actually work. A year ago, when I crafted the body, I used my wind magic to create a wind funnel testing out the functionality. I've made many, many adjustments to the body of the craft, constructing a truly aerodynamic model."

"Hmmm, I wondered about that. I'm glad you've run those tests already. Okay," Elora says decisively, stepping back so he can reach the engine pull cord. "Let's see if this thing works."

"Music to my ears." Duke walks over to her side and checks the oil and gas. He double-checks the pipes and ensures they're fitted well together with the clamps he and Elora put on. He also tests the tightness of all the other screws. The engine makes his chest swell with pride. The whole thing calls to him, and he hopes with everything in him that it works. He doesn't have high hopes for his first try, but he's excited just the same.

When his checks are finished, he looks at Elora with a grin. "Ready?"

She nods and so with a deep breath, Duke moves over to the cockpit and fingers the pull cord that should turn the engine on. He grabs it firmly, pulls...and nothing. The engine stays silent, and he hangs his head, his shoulders slumping.

Elora's hand on his shoulder is like a balm to his soul. "Don't be too disappointed that it didn't work on the first try. Come, let's take a look and see what went wrong."

Her words fuel him, and he moves around her to take a deeper look at the engine.

After pulling the cord at least twenty times and failing to start the engine, Duke gives Elora a tired look. He rubs his aching shoulder. "I think we should call it a night. We've been at this for hours, and it still won't work."

"No," she says, her eyes energized as she takes a tool, reaches into the engine and makes yet another adjustment. "I have a good feeling. Let's try again, Prince."

Unable to deny her anything, he sighs and moves back to the cord. "Okay, one last time and then we'll try again tomorrow."

She nods, her look feverish as she watches him pull down hard on the cord. The engine, in all its glory, roars to life.

Duke looks at it in amazement. With a whoop, he picks Elora up and swings her around, laughing. "It works! I can't believe it! It actually works!"

She hangs on and laughs wildly with him, but the engine chooses that moment to sputter out. Duke sets Elora down, running over to the engine.

Leaning over it he looks everything over. "The fluid wasn't circulating correctly. I think with a few modifications, we can make it run much longer. Elora," he breathes, looking at her with pride, "we did it."

She laughs, crossing her arms. "No, Prince, *you* did it. This is all your brilliant idea."

He shakes his head. "I could not have done this without you, my Little Spark. You are my muse."

Her cheeks flush pink as she looks away. "I don't know about that. Now, let's see what we need to fix to get this running longer."

They get to work and after many adjustments, they manage to get the engine running for a full thirty minutes. Finally, Duke calls it a night. "We both need our sleep. You have work tomorrow, well, later today, and I ..." he runs a hand through his hair. "need to get some sleep if I'm to face my day too."

She nods reluctantly and moves a strand of hair out of her eyes. She leaves a trail of oil on her temple. He reaches for a towel and stretches to wipe it off but then catches himself from touching her without permission. Feeling awkward, he drops his arm and hands her the towel instead.

Giving him a rueful smile, she rubs her face clean and turns to the door. "Until tomorrow night then?"

He nods and watches as she takes her cloak to walk out the door.

In less than a week's time, he hopes he can kiss her soundly goodbye when she leaves him but tonight is not that night. He can only send a prayer to the Creator that his brother works what magic he has to get Elora to the ball.

Chapter Twenty

The Maid

E lora falls into bed just as the faintest light touches the sky in the east. A thrill runs through her that the prince got his engine to run. But then she frowns. *I hate that his success will only be achieved at the expense of him hiding his true identity. He'll have to pretend to be someone else and forgo all the credit due to him.*

Rolling over to her side, she marvels at his brilliance. Despite a future together being impossible, she wants the best for him. She just can't believe he must hide his true self from the world.

She finally falls into a troubled sleep only to wake when her father shakes her shoulder. He has a worried expression. "What is it? Is it Mother?" she asks.

He nods as she jumps out of bed, hurriedly putting her wrap and mask on. "She's declined again. She needs more of the venom, I'm afraid," he whispers.

Elora was afraid of this day coming before she received the money for the rest of the medicine. In their shared excitement over the engine working, she forgot to question the prince about it last night. She'll have to find him today at the palace.

Her mother is back in her bed, and the sallow color has returned to her cheeks. Elora can only look on as her mother sleeps restlessly. She turns to her father. "I thought we'd have more time. I'll get more venom today," she says firmly. She will get the money from Duke today no matter what comes. Her bargain with him will hold. She'll just have to remind him firmly of it.

"Elora," her father says in a tired voice. "I don't know how you're planning on getting your hands on that kind of money, but be careful, my darling. I don't know what I would do if I lost you both." His eyes hold worry she wants to ease.

"That won't happen, Father. I promise you I'm perfectly safe."

With those words, she hurriedly dresses and makes her way to the palace. Not even a sharp word about her sloppy appearance from Paula detracts her from her mission to find the prince. She finds a mirror, impatiently smooths her hair back and straightening her apron. Satisfied she's presentable, she hurries up the stairs, happy to have avoided Candy's sharp eyes. She would never have gotten away this morning if her friend questioned her. It was hard enough explaining the ballroom scene.

Rushing up the stairs, she prays to find the prince quickly. Reaching the royal floor, she peers out the door from the servants' staircase, watching for Duke's eagle-eyed manservant in case he finds her away from her duties again. Seeing her way is clear, she walks down the hallway determined to find the prince. Instead of Duke, however, his brother, Harry, walks around the corner of the hallway, surprise on his face.

She's shocked when he remembers her name.

"Elora?"

Freezing in place, she can only nod.

"What a coincidence. I was just on my way to find you," he says with an easy smile.

"Me?" she squeaks, pointing to her chest.

"Yes," he says hurriedly, looking up and down the hall. He walks over to her, taking her by the elbow. "Come, let's go talk somewhere we won't be interrupted."

Why would the prince want a private conversation with her? She dumbly follows him into an empty office.

He closes the door after them, pausing for a moment with his back to her. Turning, he says, sweeping his hands wide. "As of this morning, the ball is going to be a masquerade." He gives her a wide smile.

She nods, unsure why this information is vital enough to hole her up in an office.

"And, as surprising as this sounds, I want you to attend."

She stammers, thoroughly confused. "Sir, as you are aware, my duties are to serve the royals, so I will be there."

"No," he laughs softly, looking down, then peers up at her. "Not as a servant, but as my guest."

Stunned into silence, she can only gape at him with an open mouth.

He laughs again. "I see I've shocked you. Let me explain."

She stands stiff with silence as he paces the room.

"You see, my brother has gotten himself into quite a fix. He's promised our parents he will choose a bride by the night of the ball, and he only wants one person." Prince Harry looks meaningfully at her.

She covers her mouth with her hands.

"You see, he may not have mentioned this to you, and I see he hasn't by the shock on your face, but he's come to care for you very deeply. And I'd very much like to see my brother happy. So, I'm asking you to attend the ball, to be one of the candidates for my brother's hand. You couldn't be one, you see, without attending the ball ... as a guest, of course."

Her knees feel weak, and she blindly reaches for a chair to sit down. Prince Harry quickly pulls one over, and she drops into the seat, her senses swimming. She wonders if this is some kind of grand joke and looks around the room, half expecting to see a group of nobles jumping out at her, laughing at her reaction.

When no one appears and Prince Harry looks at her expectantly, she stammers, "But how—Me? I'm not—I'd need a gown. They'll recognize me. I'm just a maid ... Me?"

Harry laughs clearly delighting in her astonishment. He leans in, seeming to relish even more this next part. "Now, this is where it gets fun. I'll provide you with a ballgown, mask, and alias. You'll be from the distant reaches of the fae lands, your family nearly forgotten nobles. The king and queen will never suspect. When the prince chooses you, you'll be a princess before they ever know anything different. We'll rush the marriage, so they don't have time to do much digging."

She swallows, her throat horribly dry. "And when they discover I'm just a maid from the palace?"

"It'll be too late for them to do anything about it. You'll already be married. They'll keep your secret to avoid a scandal."

Elora's heart races so fast she's afraid it will burst right out of her chest. "I haven't even spoken to Duke, I—I mean, the Crown Prince, about any of this. He hasn't said a word about m—marriage. How can I believe you?"

Prince Harry's eyes twinkle. "Who do you think asked to set this all up? He wants you in his life. His station unfortunately requires all of this finagling to appease the nobles and our parents. You must be at the ball."

Elora shakes her head, rising with shaking knees. "I can't. I have obligations."

"To whom?" He moves in front of the door, holding out his hands.

Swallowing to get some moisture in her throat, she whispers, "My mother, my father. Am I just supposed to just forget about them?"

Prince Harry snaps his fingers. "Oh, that reminds me." He reaches inside his waistcoat and pulls out a bottle of what appears to be liquid silver.

Elora's breath catches. *Vampire venom.* Her heart speeds even faster. She reaches out her hand just to touch it and see if it's real.

He hands it to her easily. "I believe you're in need of this?"

Holding it in her palm, she reverently caresses it. Her eyes swim with tears as she looks up at the prince. "Is this real?"

He scoffs. "Of course it is. I wouldn't give you a cheap substitute. Now, does that provide for your obligations?"

Overcome, Elora bends her head over the venom, cradling it to her chest, giving into her tears.

The prince gives her a moment before he clears his throat. "How about you give this to your sweet mother and then return here, shall we say in an hour, to plan for your debut into nobility?"

Looking up, tears trail down her face. She asks, "Did Duke organize this, too?"

He smiles gently at her. "As a matter of fact, he did. He figured out you needed the money for your mother. She has the wasting illness, doesn't she?"

His kind eyes break her even further, and the weight of hiding this great secret nearly undoes her. She covers her face and sobs into her hands. *This is enough venom to cure Mother, to save her life.*

Shaking off her weeping, she uses her apron to quickly wipe her face. "I must go. I need to give this to her." She sniffs. "She's worsened and needs it desperately."

"Of course, I'll meet you back here in an hour. We have much to do."

With one last look at the prince, she turns to the door, pocketing the precious vial. Rushing down the hallway, she marvels at what just transpired. Is she really going to try to transform into a noble lady to become a princess? It's impossible, but Prince Harry seems so confident, so sure of success, it bleeds into her thoughts. It just might work.

But does Duke really want her and only her? Why wouldn't he talk to her about it? If Prince Harry is to be believed, Duke set this entire plan into motion. Can she trust Prince Harry? From what little she knows about him, he's not to be taken too seriously, known mostly for his costly expenditures. Will this be one of them? An elaborate ball gown will not be cheap. And what about her parents? Are they to change their identities, too?

All of that flies from her mind, however, in her rush to get to her mother. She has the life-saving medication at last, and she won't stop until it's blessedly down her mother's throat.

She reaches the steps and rushes down them, feeling like she's flying. Miraculously avoiding any other servants, she pauses on the last landing before she reaches the door to the kitchens. She does not want Paula to ask why she's leaving early.

Hearing the head chef's booming voice come up from the cellar, Elora quickly passes the doorway and leaves the palace, hurrying home.

She runs all the way home, speeding past a few curious looks, and making it there quickly. Shoving open the door, she is greeted by her father's wide-eyed gaze as he carries a tray from his room. "How is she?" she asks breathlessly.

He simply shakes his head as she rushes into the bedroom. She pulls out the vial, holding it carefully. Father follows her into the room, this time his gaze showing amazement at what she holds. "Is that ..."

She nods. "Help me lift her head. She must drink this immediately."

He's at her side in the next moment, cradling her mother's head. With her teeth, she rips away the wax and then pulls the stopper out. She breathes a quick prayer to the Creator and tips the vial so the venom, a thick liquid that looks like melted diamonds, can easily slide into her mother's mouth. *Creator, please let this work!*

As the first drop of venom hits her tongue, her mother's eyes flutter and she opens her lips to receive more of the life-saving medicine. Elora complies and pours the rest into her mother's waiting mouth. *Please help her keep this down.*

Her mother swallows several times, and Elora checks to be sure none of the venom ran down her mother's cheek. No, she drank it all.

Elora leans back, and she and her father wait in suspended silence. Like magic, her mother's color returns, her cheeks and lips rosy. Her breathing eases, and an old scar on her mother's hand disappears entirely.

She looks up in wonder at her father. "Did you see that?"

He's beaming, tears trailing down his ruddy cheeks as he nods wildly. "My darling?" he calls softly. "Are you awake?"

Her mother's eyes open, clear and bright with health. She inhales deeply, looking all around. "Is it summer? It's like birds and butterflies have taken residence in my head," she says in wonder.

Elora laughs, wiping away tears that crowd her eyes. "Oh, Mother!"

Mother's laugh sounds like tinkling bells, her old vigor returned. "Oh, Elora, it's like I'm twenty years old again. Nothing hurts. I'm well!" Swinging her legs out of the bed, she moves to stand. Elora and her father back up as her mother takes her first step in months.

Elora can only look on in amazement as she watches her mother walk across the room, her legs steady, as well as the rest of her. Mother spins around, laughing loudly, and Elora joins her. Father too, they all laugh as Mother rushes to them, holding them tightly.

"I feel wonderful! It's like all my energy, my health, returned immediately. Did you give me venom? Was that the miracle I just drank?" she asks.

Elora nods wildly and hugs her mother back. She relishes feeling her healthy and whole in her arms.

Remembering Prince Harry back at the palace, she extricates herself from her family's hug, saying, "This is a terrible time, but I need to thank the prince for this; he's waiting for me."

Her mother looks at her with surprise. "Which one?"

"Which what?" Elora asks.

"Which prince, my dear? Which prince gave you the venom?"

"Harry," she says in a rush, but then corrects herself, "I mean, it's actually from the Prince Heir, Duke." Hurrying out of the room, she calls back, "It's all very confusing, I'll explain when I get back!"

Leaving her parents with so many questions isn't easy, but she must return to Harry.

She tries sneaking back into the palace, but she runs into Candy.

Candy looks all around and pulls her into a storage closet, shutting the door. "Elora! Where have you been today? Paula is having a fit. She heard you left!"

Breathless from her run back to the palace, Elora licks her lips and smiles widely. "Candy, you won't believe it. My mother is well, she's completely healthy!"

Candy eyes pop open. "How?"

"Vampire venom." Elora laughs wildly. She still can't believe what happened.

Candy is, for once, speechless. She manages her former question, "How?"

Elora blows out a breath. "That is a very long story. How much trouble am I in?"

That shakes Candy from her shocked silence. "Oh, dear, you're in quite a fix. Maybe you can sneak upstairs where you can say you've been there all this time, then you'll be fine. This is worse than when the Prince Heir kicked us all out of the ballroom."

Elora looks at her, her forehead furrowing. "Worse than that? Paula was furious, mainly because she can't argue with what a prince wants."

"I still think it was romantic," Candy says, then shakes her head. "Go, go, go."

Elora walks to the door, riding the high of excitement of her mother's miraculous healing. "Okay."

Candy jumps over and grabs Elora's arm. "Wait! Let me make sure no one is coming. If they are, I'll clear the way so you can sneak upstairs. Let's hope no one is on the servant's stairs."

Elora gives her friend a hug. "Thank you, my friend. What would I do without you?"

"Let's not think about that dismal thought. You'll always have me. Wait here. Listen at the door for me to clear your way."

Candy slips out and Elora presses her ear the door.

"No, Mistress Paula, Elora isn't down here. I truly think she's been upstairs somewhere all this time," Candy's voice rings out loudly.

A mumbled reply follows and then Candy in a loud voice continues, "But, Mistress, can I ask you a question about a shelf I saw in the pantry? It's about to fall down. It needs to be repaired immediately. All your jams are in peril, truly."

Silence follows so Elora is sure Candy has pulled Paula away from the hallway. When she's waited another ten seconds, she pulls the door open. Peeking her head out, she sees the hallway is clear.

Rushing down it, she takes the stairs, flying up them. Thankfully, she encounters no one coming down. She's breathless by the time she makes it back to the office on the royal floor.

Harry is waiting for her, with a smirk on his face. "By the glow on your face, I can see it worked."

"It did," she says with a big smile, pushing her flyaway curls away from her face. "Thank you, Prince, I'm forever in your debt."

"No, my dear, you're in my brother's debt, not mine. But that's a conversation for later. Right now, we need to get your measurements."

Just then, Elora spies a seamstress stepping away from the wall. She had completely missed the woman's presence. She gives Harry an alarmed look. *Will this woman talk about my true identity?*

Harry smiles. "Don't worry, dear. She can be trusted with seeing your face."

Then, Elora holds out her hand. "Wait a minute. First, I want to know. If this crazy scheme works, where do my parents fit in this fantasy? I'm not going to abandon them."

"Of course not, my dear. They will still be your parents."

Elora scrunches her face in confusion. "But won't they be recognized as the gardener and former maid, like me?"

Harry pats her hand. "Don't worry. We will truss them up so fancy, no one will recognize them, not even you. And if the king and queen figure out your father is their former gardener, which they won't until after the wedding, they will have to ignore it, much like ignoring your former line of work."

"Why won't they figure out my father was their gardener until after the wedding?" Elora presses. She won't risk her father being banished because of her actions.

"Because we'll keep your parents away from the royal family until after the wedding," he answers easily.

"But won't they see them at the wedding?"

Harry chuckles. "Believe me, full court dress is so extravagant, even you won't recognize them."

With that news, Elora relaxes her stiff posture, and Harry motions for the seamstress to come forward. "I still want to talk with the Prince about all of this," she says as she steps up on a stool. The seamstress tells her to hold out her arms, which she does.

"Of course you will. Just go to his little hideaway tonight and you can ask him all the questions you want."

So, Elora stands still as a seamstress takes every single measurement of her body from the tip of her head down to her toes.

Is she positive she wants to join this life? She'll marry into nobility. That's a life she's not at all familiar with. One thing is certain; she must speak with Duke.

Chapter Twenty-One

The Prince

Duke prays that Elora won't arrive early to his bunker. He needs to make his tunnel and do a test flight. All without her.

Why don't you want her here while you try out this infernal thing?

"Because if I crash, which I'm sure it will the first few times, I don't want her to worry about me, or worse, get injured from the crash," he says. "I care for her too much."

You do more than care for her, Prince.

"I do."

Admit it. Just say it once.

He swallows. He has no doubt about how he feels, but he's never said it. "I love her. More than my life." Somehow, it's freeing to finally admit it.

That wasn't so hard, was it?

"No. Now, help me."

Pushing up his sleeves, he points his hands at the area to the left of the door. It's the closest to ground level, making it easier to form a tunnel. Willing earth and wind to obey his command, he barks out to Char, "Now!"

She lands on his shoulder, and he's filled with her golden, hot energy as he pushes the dirt wall using his sizeable power. Grunting, sweat forms on his head as he shoves the earth through the ground, a distance of about ten feet. He finally breaks through but only produces a small hole. Shoring up his energy, he says to Char, "Again!" She sends another rush of raw power and he pushes with wind, manipulating earth until he has a doorway-sized hole from his bunker to the open air. Resting for a moment, he wipes his forehead and continues, trying to finish before Elora comes for the night. Everything in him wants to see her, but he must make his first few test flights alone.

By his fourth attempt, he's formed a tunnel that will get the flying craft through. He walks through his man-made hole, emerging outside into the night air. "Char, help me again, please." Once more, she sends a rush of energy, and he pushes the large pile of dirt into the earth, scattering the rest around until it was all gone. He looks around to be sure no one has seen or heard the disturbance he just created. All is clear.

He walks back inside the bunker through the tunnel, exhaustion making his vision spotty. Char flies off his shoulder, barely making it to an iron seat where she can rest. She, like him, is drained from their efforts.

I'm not sure I can fly right now.

"I know the feeling," he says tiredly, running his hand over his face. He looks up. "How about you stay here to make sure Elora gets my note?"

That sounds good. I don't really want to watch you kill yourself.

He flashes her a scowl. "I won't kill myself. It'll be fine." Hopefully.

Take your test flight and next time we'll soar the skies together.

"Fine," he says, sighing. He doesn't know how he will have the energy to complete a test flight after his exhausting task. Doggedly, he walks over to the flying machine and climbs in. Glad he's already turned off all his lamps, he puts his goggles on, situating himself in his seat.

Good luck, Prince. May the Creator watch over you and keep you safe.

He nods and considers the paper he scribbled on that lies on the table waiting for Elora. "I hope she accepts my reasons for excluding her."

If you wrote a reasonable explanation, she will understand.

"Let's hope I did." Giving the cord a firm pull, he smiles at the roar it produces, the engine sounding beautiful. Pulling the throttle toward him, the engine answers by moving the flying craft forward. Sudden exhilaration sweeps through him that his machine is working. He continues out of the tunnel.

The bunker is off the beaten path on the outskirts of the village, so he doesn't worry about anyone hearing the engine. He continues to drive the craft on the path visitors use to enter the fae city. He drives out of the forest to a flat open field. The meadow is perfect for him to gain the speed necessary to fly.

Taking a moment to breathe deeply to give himself courage, he pulls the throttle back farther to give it more power. The craft jumps to his command, and soon he's zooming on the ground as fast as a horse at full gallop. Laughing that he's going this fast, he doesn't want to waste any momentum, so he yanks the throttle back. Keeping his feet on the pedals, he whoops when the craft lifts off the ground. It rises a few feet, and he adjusts his control stick that sits between his legs, adjusting his pitch. He needs more speed to go higher. He pulls the throttle back farther and presses down on the pedals to adjust the tail to give the craft balance. But he oversteps, and the tilt to the right is too much. He's not high enough off the ground for the wing to clear the ground.

The craft pitches.

He yanks on the control stick in an attempt to level out, but it's too late. The right wing crashes. The wheels land with a slam. He jolts in his seat. He pushes the throttle to come to a stop and evaluates the state of the craft and himself.

'Whoa, that just happened. Am I okay?'

Prince? Are you okay?

Char's voice sounds afraid.

"I'm fine, Char. I'm better than fine!" Looking down at himself, he checks his fingers and limbs to make sure he can still move them. The climb out of the pilot's seat is surreal. The feel of the earth beneath his boots stabilizes him after his flight in the air. Realizing he can still walk, he takes a look at the craft. The right wing is damaged, but otherwise, the machine is unscathed.

Holding his head, he spins and laughs. He flew! Who knew such a thing could happen? He walks over to the propellers and runs his hands over them to ensure they weren't damaged in any way. Finding them in good shape, he lifts the hood of the engine. He examines it and is thrilled to find no damage.

Counting his first attempt a raging success, he jumps back in and steers the craft toward the bunker to start repairs on the wing.

Chapter Twenty-Two

The Maid

Elora makes her way to the bunker, her eyes widening when she sees an enormous hole in the ground next to the door. The prince must have used his earth and wind gifts to make this. Rushing in through the tunnel, all she can see is the darkened room. Through the hole the prince left behind, the moon gives enough light for her to find a lamp, which she quickly lights.

"He took the flying machine out without me?" she asks out loud, feeling betrayed. She looks around the abandoned room, the flying machine is gone with the prince.

A caw makes her look up, and she sees Char on one of her seats hanging off the ceiling. The phoenix flies off her perch and lands on a table, clacking a talon on a piece of paper.

"Is that for me?" she asks the phoenix.

Char cocks her head as if in answer, and so Elora walks over, picking up the note.

Little Spark,

I know you've discovered that I've taken the craft on its first flight. I didn't want to alarm you with my first failed attempts, so I'm doing this alone. I ask that you allow me to correct my mistakes on my own until I'm sure the craft is safe enough for you to fly too. Give me a few days to work out the errors I'm sure to have, and I will meet you at the masquerade. I look forward to seeing you more than anything. Thank you for trusting me with your mother's health and keeping silent about my activities. Please do not wait for me to return. I ask with a heart that cares deeply for you, and I can only hope you feel the same. If you do, you'll respect my wishes.

With love,

Duke

She gasps at the words, "With love." Does he love her? He must if he wants to marry her. *Why isn't he here so she can talk to him? And why would he go on his test flight alone?* Having no answers, she looks down to read the rest of the note.

P.S. If you worry about my safety, know that Char will be aware if anything happens to me and will come find you for help. I told her where you live, but she says she already knows, having followed you home to ensure your safety these many nights we've worked together.

Looking up at the phoenix who's watching her with eagle eyes, Elora asks, "Truly, you will know if all is well with the prince?"

Char dips her head.

Elora asks, "And is he well now?"

Char dips her head again.

Elora breathes in relief and holds the note to her chest, wondering where the prince is. Is he in the sky right now, flying above the world? Watching Char, she wishes she could speak to her to ask her these things but knows it's impossible. She's only mind-melded with Duke. Snuffing out the lamp, she leaves the bunker with heavy steps, praying to the Creator for safety over her prince.

Days pass quickly, and Elora continues her work at the palace, missing Duke more and more each day. She hadn't realized how much she valued her time with him until it was taken away from her.

She reads by the window at night in the possibility that she can spot Duke's craft gracing the night sky or in case Char comes to find her. She reads to stay awake, leaving a small lamp on by the window in her room. As she watches for the phoenix and Duke, she prays for his safety. She's on pins and needles, but she has faith that Char will find her if Duke needs her.

Plus, she's been waiting to hear more information about the ball from Prince Harry. She hates that she hasn't spoken to Duke directly about all of this, but she has no choice but to wait to see him at the ball. He's never even said he loves her, although his actions do speak for themselves. But she needs to hear them from his own lips. That she won't get the chance to see him before the masquerade is eating her up inside. But she's chosen to give Duke the time he's asked for. She could barge into the bunker hoping to catch him, but he's asked her to respect his decision to test the machine on his own, and so she must do so.

As much as it pains her to do it.

The night before the masquerade, when she comes home from work, a note is waiting for her on her bed. She opens it to find Harry has written instructions for tomorrow. She's to go to the outskirts of town to the west and wait for a carriage. It will take her to a treehouse on the other side of town, where she will get ready for the ball. She doesn't recognize the address or know who lives there, but the note is clear, and she has no choice but to follow the prince's instructions.

Not sure what to tell her parents, she decides to go with the truth. She gathers them at the kitchen table.

"Elora, you're telling us that Prince Harry has arranged for you to get all dressed up and to go to this ball?" her mother asks after Elora explains what she can.

"Masquerade," she corrects. "And yes. I'm to be in a mask, so I won't be recognized."

"Why? Why are you doing this?" Mother asks.

This is the moment she's been dreading. Telling her parents the truth about her feelings for Duke. The bargain won't allow her to talk about his project, or any part of his secret identity, but she thinks she can explain her feelings for him. "I've been seeing the Prince Heir. He's set up all of this." At their grim expressions, she takes a deep breath, gathering courage to say the rest. "Prince Harry says Duke is going to choose me as his bride."

Mother's jaw drops open and her face turns white. On the other side of the spectrum, Father's face turns red, and he rises from his chair. "Has he taken advantage of you, Elora?"

"No! No, Father. He's been a gentleman. I feel I must attend and see where all this leads."

"Even if it's to be a princess and one day a queen?" her mother asks with a strangled voice.

"And if it is? Will you support me?"

Her father retakes his seat, and both he and her mother put their hands atop hers on the table. They look at each other and after a long moment, her father finally answers, "Of course we will. We just worry that he's taking advantage of a young girl's hopes."

Her mother nods grimly.

Elora looks away. "That's not what this is. We've connected intellectually and emotionally in a way I've never dreamed of." Her father's deep frown causes her to ask, "Do you object to the prince, Father?"

"I object to any man who's not open about his pursuit of my daughter."

"I think that's what this masquerade is for. A chance to make me a lady so he can openly court and marry me."

The table falls silent.

It's her mother who says, "Well, we'll just pray your heart is protected as fiercely as you've protected me all these weeks."

Elora smiles and squeezes her hand. "I would do it over and over again if needed."

Mother smiles sadly, exchanging another look of concern with Father. She's not sure how to relieve their anxiety. Elora realizes she'll just have to go to the masquerade and see if the prince comes through on all his promises. She has to trust him in a way she's never trusted anyone before.

"I must believe that he loves me, or else he wouldn't go through all of this," she says in a small voice.

Mother frowns. "He hasn't said he loved you?"

Elora fingers the tablecloth. "Not yet."

Surprisingly, it's her father who says gruffly. "Sometimes actions speak louder than words."

Her mother gently guides the discussion to what Prince Harry is planning for Elora's masquerade ball, and Elora is grateful for the change of topic. This topic is safer.

Because she must believe that the prince is in love with her. Or else, she'll never end up at the ball.

Elora's nerves are shot as she waits on the outskirts of the west side of town for the carriage to collect her. She checks the sun in the sky to verify she's on time. She just hopes the carriage will be too.

She hears the wheels of the carriage before she sees it. It comes around the corner, and she desperately hopes the carriage is for her and not one of the many that have arrived this past week to attend the masquerade.

It comes to a stop next to her, and the driver looks over at her. "Miss Elora Wincham?"

"Yes?"

The driver nods and steps down, dropping to the ground gracefully, as most fae are. He walks to the door of the carriage and opens it, holding out his hand for her to climb the steps.

She eyes his hand, wondering if she should do this or not. She has no guarantees that the prince is offering a loveless marriage or one like one her parents have. She desperately hopes for the latter. She bites her lip.

The driver clears his throat, as if he senses her hesitation. *Duke must love me. He must. Or he wouldn't be doing all of this.* Taking a deep breath, she takes the driver's hand and climbs into the carriage. As the carriage rumbles away, she's reminded of the Cinderella story. Her story is much different, but the basics are all there. She's a maid in the palace, and Harry is acting much like a fairy godfather would. He promised in his note that he would be there while she got ready, and she's hopeful to have his presence in such a strange environment. Being waited on instead of serving a noble seems impossible.

The carriage delivers her to the treehouse, and she refers to Harry's note to see which floor she needs. She finds that she's going to the fourth level, which is the second highest.

When she climbs the stairs, she makes sure she takes the noble side and not the servants'. She breathes a sigh of relief when she knocks on the door and Harry opens it, grinning down at her. He's a little shorter than Duke, but he's still much taller than she is. He pulls her inside.

"Elora! It's time to make you a lady. Now, may I introduce my friends, Helen and Deborah? They are going to be the ones getting you ready. Ladies, this is Elora."

Elora looks at the two women and sees that Helen is a fae woman, and she's shocked to discover Deborah is a vampire.

Elora only knows because when she smiles, her sharp teeth are on display. She's never met a vampire before.

"It's nice to finally meet you." Deborah purrs.

Elora nods, looking over at Harry, wondering what he told them.

Harry gestures toward Deborah. "She's the reason your mother is feeling better."

Elora's eyes widen. "Oh!" She rushes over to her, grabbing Deborah's hand and shaking it enthusiastically. "I'd like to thank you over and over for the miraculous gift you've given to my family."

Deborah smirks, allowing her hand to be shaken. "Oh, I'm being compensated for my part. Believe me, Harry is making it quite lucrative for me."

Elora drops her hand, turning to Harry. "Do I owe you money for this?"

"No, my dear," Harry drawls. "She doesn't mean money. She means I'll owe her in favors, which in the political world are just as valuable. Don't worry. I didn't promise anything I wasn't willing to. Besides, Duke insisted, so here we are."

Helen approaches in a no-nonsense manner. "Well, now that introductions are out of the way, we really do need to get started. It looks like we have much to do." She fingers Elora's hair and grimaces.

"It's clean," Elora protests.

"It's not the cleanliness that concerns me," Helen says with a frown. "It will need a cut and shaping."

"Won't my hair be pinned up?"

"My dear, there's no point arguing with these particular women," Harry says with a chuckle. "What they have to do is all necessary for you to fit in with the noble class."

Elora concedes and submits herself to whatever the women have planned. "Will Duke escort me to the masquerade?" she asks hopefully.

Harry's smile falters. "We have to stick to the story that he's meeting you at the dance. So, no, I'm afraid it will have to be me."

She nods, trying to hide her disappointment.

Deborah and Helen kick Harry out of the treehouse so they can get to the womanly tasks, but he promises to return to collect Elora in time for the ball.

Elora spends the next three hours enduring all kinds of unheard of, but seemingly luxurious, beauty treatments. Mud baths apparently soften skin. They ruthlessly pluck most of her eyebrows and apply bright purple plants on her lips and cheeks, plumping them up. Worse, they rip off all the hair on her arms with wax strips. Elora barely recovers from that when Deborah mercilessly cuts off six inches of her hair. The vampire then smooths it into submission with a hot iron before adding curls. Piece by piece, they layer her hair up on her head, piling her long tresses into an elaborate updo. Between Helen and Deborah, they give Elora's fingernails a total makeover, both of them tsking over the state of them. They put cream after cream on her skin to soften the calluses formed from hard work at the palace. Her new friends apply more makeup than Elora knew existed. She wonders if she'll even recognize herself when they're done.

Will the Prince?

When it comes time for the grand finale, to finally see her ballgown, Elora is more exhausted than she's ever been before. Dressed in a silk robe, she rubs her smooth arms nervously as Deborah and Helen remove a glorious gown from its protective bag.

Elora gasps when she sees it. It's a white and gold masterpiece with golden threads embellished in a menagerie of leaves and flowers. It falls to the floor and looks more majestic than anything she's seen before.

"We got our hands on this a week ago and barely had time to fit it to your measurements," Helen says proudly as she looks the gown over. "Ready to put it on?"

Elora nods, suddenly energized with the thought that this magical night is happening. She just might get her waltz with the prince after all.

They dress her carefully, first having her step into a chemise and stockings. A corset then sucks all the breath out of her. But it's worth it because as soon as she dons a hoop, they lower the gown over her head. The sweetheart neckline is lower than anything she's dared to wear before, but Helen and Deborah insist it's in the right style. Thanks to the corset, the dress fits like a dream. Elora's afraid to even touch the dress, marveling at the intricate needlework that makes it look like she wears a golden garden. Delicate gold slippers are put on her stockinged feet, long white gloves slipped on her hands, and she's finally declared ready.

They wouldn't allow her to look in a mirror all day, and so when she finally looks at her reflection in a full-length mirror, she gasps. Her corset makes her breathless to do so, but she can't help her reaction. A lovely young lady with golden eyes, which are accentuated with smoky grey eye makeup, stands in front of the mirror. She has to raise a hand to prove that it's her.

"You're beautiful. We see what the prince likes in you. And it's not just your beauty," Deborah says, "You put up with our treatments all day without a single complaint. You will make a lovely queen."

"If he chooses me," she says shyly, lowering her darkened lashes. *What if he changes his mind and picks someone else?*

"He will choose you," Deborah says confidently. "He's crazy not to."

Helen nods, smiling.

Just then, someone knocks on the door in a strange series of knocks.

"That's Harry." Deborah rushes to the door. Before she fully opens it, she warns him, "Be prepared to be surprised."

When he walks in and spies Elora, his eyebrows rise impressively. "My dear, I mean, Lady Thompson, you look absolutely stunning. And I'm saying that objectively. My brother will be absolutely tongue tied when he sees you."

"This is all thanks to you. I can't imagine what this dress cost." She blinks back tears.

"Oh, no, you don't. You're not going to cry and ruin our hard work." Helen dabs at Elora's eyes with a cloth. "And don't worry about what Harry chooses to spend his money on. Believe me, we never do. He usually doesn't pay a dime."

Harry winks at her. "Favors, remember? Now it's time to go."

"Wait! You forgot her mask!" Helen cries. She steps up, producing an ornate white and gold mask that is as beautiful as the dress. It has gold scrolls that curl around Elora's eyes, making her look mysterious and alluring.

"Sorry, I'm not very good at this godfather business. Now you're ready." He offers his arm, which she accepts. He nods at her in approval and leads her out the door.

Saying goodbye to Helen and Deborah, after thanking them profusely, she steps carefully down the steps. Prince Harry has a carriage waiting for them. It's more elaborate than the one that picked her up, and she holds her breath as he helps her inside.

How is this her life? She really is in a fairytale.

On the way to the castle, Prince Harry dons a simple black mask and coaches Elora to follow his or Duke's lead on dinner forks and spoons. Fortunately, she's laid many a dinner table, so she should have no problems with that part of the evening. And as far as introductions, Harry tells her to let him take the lead on who she interacts with. He will raise his eyebrows if she's to respond to a conversation. If he doesn't give her this sign, she's to acknowledge the person with a nod, but not to answer. It's one thing observing social rules, it's another to perform them. She feels quite lost about the social graces and will entirely rely on Prince Harry to guide her through those waters.

"Now, remember, you're from the border of the Lumiara mountains. Your family is an old noble one, the Thompsons.

Your parents are not here; you're attending alone as my guest, an old friend of the family. We haven't seen each other since we were young."

She files all the information away, and before she knows it, the coach rolls up to the palace. They wait only a short while before it's their turn to disembark. As the footman opens the carriage door and offers his hand to help her climb from the carriage, curious eyes turn her way. Fae men and women outside the castle stop talking before leaning into each other, glancing at her, and whispering furiously.

"You're already a topic of conversation. Good. The bigger entrance you make, the more believable it will be for my brother to take notice of you," Harry says in a low tone. "Of course, you're with me, so you're automatically interesting."

She smiles at his lack of humble behavior.

A young fae man with a dark blue mask, who was in the path of her smile, takes it as an encouragement to approach. He walks up to Prince Harry, grinning at Elora as he bows. "Lord Ellington at your service." She looks to Harry, but he doesn't give her the sign.

So, she nods regally but does not respond, which seems very rude, but Lord Ellington just smiles, bows, and walks away.

Harry squeezes her arm in encouragement and leads her inside. Walking up the noble staircase is an experience in itself. Harry nods at the nobles who loiter on the stairs, waiting for introductions. Harry stops to briefly talk to several of his young male friends. During those conversations, many of the nobles who had whispered at her entrance look her over curiously as they pass by on the stairs. Harry ignores them all, so she does too.

Harry leans in when they're finally alone climbing the stairs and whispers furiously, "Please tell me you know how to dance."

She smiles. "Yes, I begged my mother to teach me all the dances."

He relaxes. "Good. I don't know how I would have spun that if you didn't."

They finish climbing the stairs and arrive at the level where the ballroom is. It takes up the entire floor; the enormous room suddenly intimidating her. This had always been just another room to clean, but now she must navigate its social waters as an elegant young lady.

A gasp has her swinging her head to the right. Candy stands with her mouth gaping open, holding a platter of drinks. The tray tips precariously. She stares openly at Elora.

Elora gives her head a tiny shake. Her palms sweat in her gloves. *Will Candy give her identity away before she's even walked into the ball?*

Candy gives Elora an awed, big smile and rushes away with her tray pinched between her fingers.

Elora breathes easier.

Harry cocks his head toward Elora. "Close one," he says in a low tone.

She nods.

He leads her to approach the massive doors that open up to the already large crowd. "Are you ready?" he says under his breath.

Her heart is hammering so wild in her chest she's afraid it'll rob her of all her oxygen. She takes short quick breaths, trying not to panic. "What would you do if I said no?" she asks just as quietly.

He stiffens next to her. "It's a little late to back out now, Princess."

"I'm not a princess yet," she whispers.

"Well then, let's make you one, Lady Thompson. It's your time to shine." He gently pulls her forward.

She can only hope to dazzle as spectacularly as her dress. Prince Harry is right. As soon as they step up to the door, all eyes turn to her. She's handed a dance card by the butler, who mercifully doesn't look twice at her.

And she steps into a dream.

Chapter Twenty-Three

The Prince

As Duke watches the door to the ballroom, rumors wildly spread of a mysterious fae woman whose beauty far surpasses any other in the room. He has no doubt they're speaking of Elora. They're all wondering who she is.

He knows it's his Little Spark, dazzling as she goes.

All eyes are on him since everyone at the ball has found out about his need to find a bride by tonight. Everyone wants to see who Duke will favor. But the moment Elora sweeps in on his brother's arm, everything in the room stops moving except for her. It's like time freezes, and he wouldn't forget this moment in a million years. He could care less the whole ball is watching him.

When she stops and looks around, he knows she's looking for him, and that makes him inordinately proud. Even with her mask on, he would know her anywhere. It's everything from the curve of her cheek that the mask doesn't hide, to her dress that fits her perfectly. He could never forget her curves and this dress hugs every one just right. And the way she carries herself, it's as if she's already his queen. She walks as if she's floating on a cloud, which befits her as a future ruler.

He doesn't recall who he's talking to, but at this moment it doesn't matter. He excuses himself and walks directly over to her. Several nobles step into his path, however, and he has to extricate himself from their conversations before he looks to see Harry leading Elora away from him. She still looks all around the room, searching for him. Why would Harry take her in the opposite direction?

To prolong the moment. Char provides unhelpfully. *People have their eyes on you, and they've already seen you notice her.*

Biting back curses, he continues making his way through the throng of people toward Elora. He watches as several noblemen approach Harry and Elora, and he's supremely satisfied to see Harry continue to walk and not talk to any of the men.

Just then, Elora finally turns her head toward him. Their eyes lock and everything else disappears. He's walking, but he's not sure he remembers putting one step ahead of another. Other guests become statues, mere obstacles in front of his prize.

She waits for him, her gold eyes never leaving his as he makes his way to her.

He can't take his eyes off this heavenly creature.

Finally, he reaches her. Bowing low, he turns to Harry, waiting for a proper introduction.

Harry smiles and obliges. "Crown Prince Duke Williams, do you remember our old family friend, the Lady Elora Thompson?"

Duke could crow for joy. His brother came through on all his promises and gotten Elora here. "It's very nice to see you again, Lady Thompson."

Elora nods with an elegant tilt of her head. Duke reaches for her gloved hand and kisses the knuckles lightly, subtly rubbing his lips on them, making her shiver. Thrilled to have her here in this ballroom, he rises and asks, "Lady Elora, may I have your first waltz?"

She smiles beautifully and nods, producing her dance card. With the attached pencil, he signs his name for the first dance of the night as well as the Luriel. He signs his name for all the waltzes. He won't stand by and watch her dance any of those with anyone else. He knows what he's doing by dancing more than two dances with an unmarried young woman. He's making a claim. He looks up at her, smiling. "I hope I can resurrect fond memories with my selection."

Demurely, she reviews her card, and her eyes widen. Then her lips curl up deliciously. "I'm honored, my Prince."

The opening strains of the waltz fill the room, and every eye turns to him. He's expected, as the heir to the kingdom, to open the dances. He smiles and holds out his hand to Elora.

Her hand shakes slightly as she puts it in his. He squeezes it, encouraging her and leads her onto the dance floor. He places one hand on her slim waist and holds out his hand for her to place her hand in it. He casts his eyes over the rare beauty in his arms. Truly, his brother has somehow made her even more lovely. She's always been beautiful, but tonight she shines with the brilliance of a star. He still prefers her hair unbound and wild around her shoulders. But he has to admit, all of it piled on her head and cascading down her neck in curls is about to undo him. He wants to kiss every single place the curls touch her elegant neck.

She smiles at him, and he leads her in the first dance, entirely captivated. He hasn't even had a chance to tell her how he feels about her. He's never felt a moment more fitting than to say it now. By selecting her for the first dance of the night, he's announced his intention that he favors her. His behavior toward her the rest of the night will only confirm his choice: Elora.

He pulls her closer to him as he swings her around the dance floor. The rest of the nobles join them, and soon they're surrounded by dancing couples. They only serve as the background. He leans in, whispering in her ear, "I love you, Little Spark. I want to treasure you for the rest of my life."

He leans back, his eyes searching hers. They're beautiful as they glitter behind her mask, bright with tears. They look like gold coins. "Are you sure?"

He pulls her closer. "I wouldn't have gone through all this to get you here otherwise."

Tears fill her eyes. "I love you, too. And not just because of all of this. I just love you."

He catches a tear from her eyelash. "No more tears, Little Spark. Never again."

"I can't promise that."

"Well, promise me that I'll know about all of them."

She smiles softly as he twirls her around the floor.

"I just wish..." she starts to say.

"What? Tell me what you want, and I'll do everything I can to make it happen."

She laughs lightly, looking all around, as if she's just now noticing all the other couples dancing around them. "As if you haven't done enough."

"I'd do far more. Give me the word. Become my bride, and I'll shower you with every single star you wish upon. Your wishes will be my commands."

She blushes and looks down. They continue their dance, but he knows it will soon be ending. He must know her answer. She looks up, her eyes shining. "Yes, my prince. I will marry you. But I ask one thing."

"Anything."

She bites her lip, distracting him for a moment. "Tell the world who you truly are. Don't hide behind a shell of a man. Be yourself. You have value as an inventor. Just because you're a prince doesn't mean you can't do what you love."

The notes to the waltz end, and he stops, stunned by her request. He knows that's how she's always felt, but she doesn't understand his world. He would give her anything but that. The royal court would never accept his true identity. He *wants* them to know. He would give anything to reveal himself, but they'll never accept it, accept *him* as an inventor and a king.

Reading his answer with his fallen expression, she steps back and curtsies low. "I thank you for the lovely dance, my Prince." Her expression is crestfallen, but she quickly hides it. A determined look comes over her. What is she thinking?

Having no answer, he leads her off the dance floor, his heart pounding. Her request raises a question in him he's never considered. Would his parents and the nobles accept him? And then, worse, would Elora refuse to marry him if he doesn't do it? His heart pounds at the thought of a life without her.

He delivers her to Harry and, swallowing to get moisture in his throat, he asks her, "May I get you a cup of punch?"

No! Don't leave her like that! Char screams in his mind.

She nods with a strained smile on her face.

Now that he's offered punch, he must fulfill her wish to have one. As he walks away, he thinks, 'What is she thinking? Is he losing her before his eyes?'

Yes, you dolt! Don't leave things like that!

Harry looks at him, a question in his eyes. Duke shakes his head curtly and turns in the direction of the refreshment table. Walking, he turns over her request in his mind, examining it from every angle. He would lead his country one day, and he won't fail in that. But what is the harm in admitting to doing something he loves?

Nothing! She's right!

He collects two glasses of punch and returns to Harry only to find Elora missing. "Where is she?" He looks over to the dance floor to see if she's dancing. When he doesn't find her, he turns to Harry.

"Relax. She said she was going to freshen up. She's in the powder room."

He nods, doing as his brother suggests. "You've done us a great service, Harry. Thank you."

Harry chuckles. "Don't thank me yet. You still have to announce her as your bride before the night is done."

Duke smiles. "She's just told me she loves me and will marry me. I will make my announcement at the end of the ball."

Harry looks him over. Duke wears his royal white suit with a red sash announcing his status as the royal heir. "Well, look at you. Finding true love. Lucky man."

Duke's chest swells. "I truly am. I will do everything in my power to make her happy." His conscience twinges that he turned down her one request. Can he be the man she wants him to be?

I agree with Elora. Reveal who you really are.

As time passes and Elora doesn't return from the ladies' room, he turns to Harry. "Let's look for her. Maybe something's wrong."

Harry scoffs. "What could happen in a water closet?"

Duke doesn't want to think about the hidden alcoves in the ballroom she could have been dragged into. He sets down the punch and directs Harry to go in one direction, while he goes in another.

He had just searched one of the many balconies when a shrill voice meets his ears.

"Oh, Prince? Prince?"

He attempts to ignore her by keeping his back turned, but Lady Mary circles into his path.

"Prince? You must not have heard me call for you. I am so happy to find you out here. I've always found the night air to be so romantic, wouldn't you agree?"

If she were a man, he would have shoved past and forgotten the moment ever happened, but she's a lady, so he stays and grits out with clenched teeth, "No, Lady Mary, actually I don't."

"Oh?" She moves in closer, waving her fan all around.

He couldn't care less what her blasted fan is communicating, he needs to continue searching for Elora.

"Well," she says in a breathy tone as she steps even closer. "Then tell me where your favorite romantic places are, and I'll gladly visit them."

Tired of her games, he says in a firm tone, "There is nowhere in the entire world of Lurin you can induce me to stay with you, Lady Mary. Now, if you'll excuse me." Since she had moved even closer, he only has to take one step to move around her and stalk back into the ballroom.

All thoughts of Lady Mary fly from his mind as he continually comes up empty in his search. He knows one thing. He will find his bride. And if she's in trouble, someone will pay.

Chapter Twenty-Four

The Maid

Elora directs her steps, never feeling surer about anything. She's leaving the ballroom, but it's not to escape the Prince. It's to save him. She doesn't want to watch him hide a piece of himself that's so important to him. So, she's doing the one thing she knows to do to force him to admit it.

He'll thank her for it later. Hopefully.

The noble staircase is empty, thank the Creator. Everyone is enjoying the masquerade, so she encounters no one as she picks up her voluminous skirts and steps down as quickly as she can. Elora strains to make out the carriage that brought her here. She needs to get home and out of this dress. What she's going to do will require all of her concentration, and being in a ballgown will not aid her.

Once she's off the staircase, she looks down the line of carriages and finds Prince Harry's easily. She's thankful it's ostentatious enough to recognize. She rushes over to it, ignoring the curious stares of the coach drivers she passes.

When she reaches the Prince's coach, she asks breathlessly. "Can you take me where I need to go?"

The coach driver stammers, "Of...of course, my lady. I'm to take you anywhere you need."

She leans in and whispers her address, and his eyes widen. She doesn't want any of the other drivers hear her say the address. Climbing in, she hopes with wild abandon that Duke will forgive her for doing this. But she must.

As the coach drives her home, she squeezes her fingers together, trying not to let any doubt change her mind.

The coachman reaches her home, and he helps her down from the carriage. By this time, twilight will happen soon. She needs to hurry.

She flings open the door, startling her parents.

"Elora, my dear, look at you." A glowing wonder fills Mother's expression. "What are you doing here? Why aren't you at the ball?"

Elora walks briskly into her room. "Mother, please help me out of this dress. I must go quickly. There's something I must do."

Mother follows her into the room and, when Elora turns her back, dutifully starts unlacing her dress. "Elora, what are you doing?"

"I can't explain. Not right now. I've made a bargain I can't get out of. Just know I feel that I'm doing the right thing."

Mother works quickly, and soon the beautiful dress is unlaced. Elora slips out of it, reaching inside her dresser for a plain working dress. She dresses in it, and when she looks in the mirror, she realizes she's still wearing her mask. She had completely forgotten about it. Taking it off, she frowns at her reflection in her elaborate updo. It will take too much time to undo all of it, so she leaves it.

She turns to leave, but her mother is standing in front of the door, her arms folded in front of her. "I hope you've thought carefully through what you're doing, Elora. You could be wasting a wonderful opportunity."

Elora straightens her spine. "I have, Mother. Believe me. I know what I'm doing." *Well, sort of.* "Please trust me."

Mother nods slowly and moves away from the door. "May the Creator go before you."

Elora rushes past her and leaves the room, passing her bewildered father as she exits their home. She rushes down the stairs and runs a full sprint to the underground bunker. She's out of breath by the time she reaches it. She sees that the prince has fashioned a door with a large piece of canvas to cover the hole. It's so far out of the way no one will look twice at it.

She tears down the canvas, throwing it over to the side.

Once the tunnel is clear, she runs inside, finding Char sitting on one of her iron seats. She watches her intently, and Elora says, "Char, I'm going to fly this plane. I'm hoping the Prince will admit to it being his creation. Please don't tell him my plans; just tell him that I love him, but I cannot marry a man who would live a lie. Please tell him if he loves me, he'll do the right thing."

Char looks at her, her tail flaring up in flames. It's clear she's agitated.

Climbing into the plane's seat, Elora puts the goggles on that she finds on the seat. "I'm sorry, dear Char. Just pray I don't kill myself."

Elora gives a firm yank to the cord. The engine roars to life. *Thank the Creator!* She runs over in her mind the construction of the craft and all the prince's instructions on how to fly it. This is absolutely insane for her to try this, but she thinks she can do it. She knows everything there is to know about this machine. And she knows the Prince has made the necessary modifications now that he's flown it several times for it to work well. She slides down the seat to reach the pedals and finds that they reach her feet. Duke must have made sure they would reach her shorter legs when she wanted to fly. Well, that time is now.

She puts one hand on the throttle and the other on the control stick. The throttle has tension when she touches it, and she remembers this will make the propellers spin faster. The control stick moves easily in her hand, with much less resistance.

Creator, please protect me!

Char squawks, flying around the plane, her whole body now in flames.

"I'll be fine," she calls over the engine's noise. "I think."

She looks over the wings and sees they've both been repaired. The prince must have crashed during his test flights. With her heart in her throat, a numbing fear climbs through her throat at the very real chance she will crash too. *I will not think like that. I will do this.* She's going to fly the machine over the ballroom, and she can only hope once she lands, if she lands safely, the prince will take credit for this wondrous thing. She's half afraid that Duke will give her all the credit. But she can only hope he won't.

"This is crazy, pure madness." At those words, she reaches to pull the throttle back, turning on the propellers and making the craft move forward.

She drives the machine out of the tunnel. She knows of a field big enough to gain the speed that will make it fly. Char follows her out, putting out her flames and Elora is relieved Char's not so upset but also that she won't be alone in this.

The engine rumbles loudly as she drives, and Elora prays harder than ever before.

She reaches the field early enough that she knows the machine will attract attention from fae who are out and about. Twilight is upon them, but there's still light to see. Even if there wasn't, she would have gone anyway. And the more attention she garners right now, the better.

Taking a bracing breath, she pulls the throttle back further, picking up speed as the wheels bounce over the grass. Char flies next to her, keeping up easily. Well, these will be two secrets of Duke's out, unless Char hides herself soon. Elora has to acknowledge the very real fact that if Duke doesn't step up and admit to this being his creation, she will have to claim it. To save her arm, she can't say anything about Duke's activities. She just hopes this doesn't count as revealing them. She can only pray for the phoenix's safety too. Knowing better than to think she could control the majestic phoenix, Elora concentrates on what she's doing. She keeps the control stick steady as she picks up speed.

She's going faster, and she can't help but feel a huge thrill. Just then, the craft lifts off the ground for a moment, and she squeaks a scream at the exhilarating feeling of being weightless.

The nose of the craft grows higher, and she rises in the air. Char keeps up with her, flying to her right. Twilight lights up the sky in a cascade of colors, and she can't believe she's soaring through it.

Laughing delightedly, Elora keeps the craft level with the control stick maneuvering it. She presses on the left pedal when she feels herself tipping to the right. The craft balances out and continues to rise, and she flies over the treetops. Experimenting with turning, she pulls the control stick to the left, and the craft immediately obeys, steering her to the left. But she turns too hard, because the left wing dips and skims the top boughs of the trees. She yelps and pants. She pulls the control stick hard to the right, and the machine wobbles. Char squawks at her and Elora uses the pedals to balance the craft. Her heart hammers at the near devastating mistake. Once level, she keeps a gentle but firm hand on the control stick so that doesn't happen again. She takes deep breaths, trying to catch her breath.

Char squawks again, and Elora sees her flying toward the palace. The phoenix is pointing her in the direction of where to find Duke.

Elora follows as Char flies ahead of the craft. The wind blows in her face, her hair unraveling. Elora exalts in the feeling that she's actually flying! This is an act that only Char had been able to do, now she and Duke. She flies in a straight pattern, not wanting to make any more disastrous turns. She feels as if she's on a plain of grass, but instead, she's in the sky. And suddenly she has a name for this machine: an airplane. It's like she has command of the skies, and she hopes Duke likes the name.

Shouts sound below her, and she knows she's got the attention of the town. Looking down, she sees a crowd of people craning their necks up at her, pointing and shouting.

She keeps a good hold of the control stick, and soon the palace is in her sights. Blowing out a nervous breath, Elora worries the fae soldiers will shoot Char down. She's relieved to see Char drop and hide in the trees, allowing Elora to go on alone. She mourns the only place she can land the plane when she's done with her flight: her father's garden.

Shouts ring out when the nobles standing on the balcony balk in surprise at her approach. Elora can only imagine what she looks like, but she hopes she doesn't appear threatening. Her hair now flies behind her in a long banner announcing to the world a woman is flying the airplane. The nobles on the balcony crouch as she flies over them. She flies to the other side of the palace, the same scene repeating on the balcony there. Screams and alarmed cries fill the air, and she looks down to see if Duke is one of them. She flies by too quickly to see him. Carefully steering the craft around so she circles the palace, the nobles stream out onto all the balconies and down the staircases, using even the servants' staircase to get a good look at her flying.

By now, fae from the neighboring treehouses line their staircases to get a look at her flight too.

Hoping Duke is out, it's now or never to get his attention. She circles the palace, watching for him, and spotting his red sash, she knows right when he sees her. She's close enough to see his shocked expression. But then she realizes it's not just shock; he looks *angry*.

He's probably worried about her flying. She wonders too what he thought when she left the ballroom without a word. He's probably been worried sick about her.

Having made her point, she aims the airplane toward the gardens, ready to land and face the prince. She hopes desperately that all of this does what she set out to do.

She tries easing the lever down, realizing this is the most dangerous part of her flight. Any wrong move and she'll crash into the ground. But when she pushes on the control stick to point the plane down, it won't move. She can move it in every direction but down. She uses more of her strength, but she can't get it to move. It's jammed.

At this worst possible moment, the engine starts smoking. From flying for so long? Terror swarms all her senses. She's sure she's taxed the engine too much. Fear careens through her, and she looks down wildly, searching Duke out. She finds him still on the balcony, his expression now one of horror.

She tries to communicate how sorry she is. She's not going to survive her first flight after all.

Chapter Twenty-Five

The Prince

Duke can only watch in terror as Elora battles the aircraft. *Why isn't she landing?* She seems to be struggling with the lever. She can't land. And now the engine is smoking.

He calls out to Char. She's nearby, hiding in the trees. He turns to her in relief. She flies toward him and shouts sound all around.

A soldier points his crossbow at his pet. "It's a phoenix!"

"No!" Duke lunges and smacks down the weapon. "She's mine," he snarls.

Char keeps her flames tucked away and continues her flight toward him.

Duke, she needs you!

"I know, fly me up to her!"

Arrows fly toward Char from other soldiers he didn't command. He spins, holding his arms out. "Don't shoot!" Several soldiers lower their crossbows, uncertain on what to do. "She's not to be harmed."

He turns to Char. She flies straight toward him and banks when she reaches him. He jumps, grabbing onto her clawed feet. She squawks a cry. Now that they're connected, he'll use his wind to help her fly, but he hopes she can carry most of his weight. Like what she did with him for the tunnel, he fuels her with hot, golden energy. Using Duke's wind to help propel her, Char heads toward the craft that's now flying at a tilt. Elora is still fighting with the lever. He just needs to reach her.

Char struggles, flapping her wings wildly to keep them aloft, so he squeezes his eyes shut, gifting her more energy. His vision gets spotty, but he continues feeding her his strength.

With a cry, Char flies with powerful thrusts of her wings. They finally reach Elora. Char flies level with the craft, so Duke can reach in.

"Duke! I can't get the stick to move down!" Elora cries.

"Don't worry, I've got you!" In a crazy act of faith, he lunges for the side of the craft. He lets go of Char and grabs on, hanging by the side with one hand.

"Duke!" Elora screams, holding onto him while trying to steer too. Reaching up, he grabs the side with his other hand and pulls himself up. He folds his upper body into the cramped cockpit, bracing his leg on the right wing. Upside down, he reaches for the bottom of the control stick. He heaves, yanking it back. It doesn't move. Fear roars through him, he yanks on it again. It still doesn't move. *Creator, help me! I'll go down with Elora; I won't abandon her. Please help me get this moved.* Inhaling deeply, he uses all his strength to pull it as hard as he can. It releases. He lets out a shout of relief. The problem is that the stick obeys his command and tips the craft down. He falls into Elora's lap, and she loses her grip on the control stick.

The machine dips, and he pushes himself out of Elora's lap so she can reach for the control stick again. He moves to the side and braces his leg on the wing while his arms hold himself up. His arms shake as he balances himself on the side of the craft.

It totters while she rights the craft. He holds himself as still as he can, but she struggles. His weight is too much for the small craft.

"Elora," he calls over the wind and roar of the engine. "You're going to have to land this now; this can't bear us both. Keep it level!"

Smoke pours from under the hood. He calls for Char in his mind.

Elora nods in two jerks.

Char is at his side in the next moment.

Get on!

He reaches with one hand and grabs Char's foot. Once he has it, he lets go of the smoking craft and clings to both her feet. Char drops in the air, her wings straining as she flaps wildly to hoist them up. Duke commands the wind to push them up and stop their freefall. He digs deep and infuses her with his near empty reserve of energy. Char uses it to power her flight.

Hang on! I'll take you down.

She slows her descent by spreading her wings out and gliding in tight circles. They near the ground, and when he's close enough, Duke drops.

Dizzy from Char's descent, he finds where Elora is. She's now able to direct the craft down, and he prays she keeps it level.

Heart racing, panic robs Duke of breath as she gets closer to the ground. Trees hide her from view and he runs in her direction, Char keeping up with him. He doesn't think of anything but prayers that Elora makes it down safely. Landing is the hardest part of flying.

Please, Creator, don't let her crash into a tree. Help her find level ground.

Lungs burning, he races toward where he last saw Elora. He doesn't hear a crash, so he holds hope that she's safe. Racing toward a clearing, he watches as Elora directs the craft, but it's tilting too far to the right. "Straighten it out, Elora!"

The craft balances itself at the last moment and glides into a near-perfect landing. Racing toward her, he runs beside the craft as it slows down. As soon as it's stopped, he reaches into the craft and pulls her out, hugging her tightly. "Elora, Elora! Are you all right?" He buries his face in her neck, hardly believing she made it down safely. He pulls back, holding her face in his hands. "What were you thinking? Why did you do such a crazy thing? Char said it was for my own good. What did you mean?"

"I'm sorry," she keeps repeating, squeezing him back. She sobs and he crushes her to him again.

Char joins them, landing on his shoulder. She nudges Elora with her beak, checking her over.

She did well, Prince.

He can only nod as he breathes in Elora's unique scent. By now darkness has descended, but a crowd bearing torches surrounds them, all the fae talking loudly. Moonlight shines on the product of his last two years where smoke leaks from the hood.

"Are you alright?"

"What is this thing?"

"Is that a phoenix?"

More questions fill the air, but Duke, his heart still hammering in his chest, just holds Elora to him, thanking the Creator over and over that she's safe.

Trumpets sound, and Duke groans. His parents are coming. They're going to want an explanation. And he hasn't talked to Elora about her wild plan.

Prepare yourself, Prince.

He blinks back tears as he looks over Elora's head at Char. "Thank you, dear friend. You saved Elora."

Of course I did. Did you ever doubt my abilities?

He laughs. "Of course not."

Elora reaches up tentatively, and Char turns her attention to the woman in his arms. Elora runs her hand reverently over Char's bright red feathers. "You saved me," she says in awe.

Char dips her head in acknowledgement and wraps her tail feathers around Elora's shoulders in a kind of hug.

Elora giggles.

Needing answers, Duke holds Elora at arm's length and shakes her gently. "Why did you do this? What could possibly be your reason?"

She looks up at him with moist eyes. "You can't guess?"

He presses his lips together. He can't believe her bravery just so he can claim this flying machine.

"Son, what is the meaning of this?" the King roars. "What is that thing? And who is this?" His heavy form walks up to them in angry steps. He huffs, his exertion evident. The Queen is next to him.

Pulling in a breath to steady his frayed nerves for what he's about to do, he gives Elora's shoulders a squeeze before he pulls her to his side, keeping her there to face his parents. Char stays on his shoulder, and for once, he's glad of her presence. But he watches closely for any type of attack on his dear pet.

His mother and father stand before him, both of them out of breath, their eyes wide and mouths gaping open. They watch Char warily, their postures stiff, then run their gazes over the flying machine. Harry runs to catch up with all of them. His mouth is like a gaping fish as he looks between Duke, Elora, Char, and the flying craft.

Duke starts, "Father, maybe we should discuss this in private..."

"We will discuss this *now*!" his father interrupts, his face mottled red. He gestures toward the soldiers, commanding them, "Move this crowd back. I want a private audience with my son. And bring me some light."

Several soldiers bear torches and surround them while the others move the fae back so the royal family can speak.

Once they have relative privacy, the king turns to Duke and Elora. "Is that what I think it is?" he gestures at Char.

Duke nods and says in a hard voice, "Char is mind-melded to me. She's a phoenix and will *not* be harmed."

"You have broken the law. You do not decide that bird's fate."

"It is not against the law to have a pet phoenix, Father; you know that full well."

The king splutters, "Well then I'll make it one!"

"You do that and I will abdicate my position. She is as a part of me as my arm."

The king presses his lips together in a white line, his face turning redder. He turns his furious gaze on the craft. "Well, then, explain what *that* is."

"It's a flying machine," Duke answers.

"An airplane," Elora corrects, looking up at him with a small smile.

He likes that name. He squeezes her shoulder. He nods. "Yes. It's an airplane."

"Who built this?" his father asks, directing his question at Elora.

She rubs her arm, which is probably burning in warning. She can't answer his father, or she'll lose her hand.

"I did," Duke says in a firm voice. "Elora assisted me." He's surprised he doesn't say it only to save Elora's hand, but because he suddenly *wants* them to know. Power courses through him as he finally conquers his lack of courage.

Both the king and queen inhale sharply at his admission.

"Are you telling me," his mother whips out, "that *you* are responsible for this ... thing?" She looks at the airplane with distaste.

Duke stands tall. "Yes. I am an inventor. I've been building this in an underground bunker for the past two years."

His father splutters, "What? This...this is *yours?*"

Ignoring the king, the queen asks, "And you felt you had to hide this from us? Why?" Her steel gaze looks wounded for a moment before it's gone.

Duke looks at her with disbelief. "Mother, I'm supposed to do one thing, and that is to manage the rule of this country, but I wasted half my life courting the nobles."

Her gaze sharpens. "You were to rule the country by learning about your nobles through social events. That is wasting your life?"

Duke sighs. "No. But I was tired of pretending to laze my days away, like a true indolent prince heir would do. I wanted to do something else with my life. Would you have supported me in my endeavor to build this?"

"Absolutely not," she grinds out. "But I don't like being lied to." She looks away.

Duke stiffens. "I never once lied to either of you. But I was determined to create this one-of-a-kind invention, and I knew I would not have your support."

"*When* could you possibly have had time to do this?" she whips out, turning back to him.

"Mostly while everyone slept."

"So, you pretended to laze your mornings away, but instead you were sleeping because you were up all night," his mother said.

"And I'd do it all over again the same way."

She falls silent at his words, seeming to mull them over.

His father, on the other hand, blusters, "Well, you assumed right. We need your attention on our family, our country, not on fanciful inventions, such as this ... monstrosity."

Duke stifles his curse. "Do you not realize the import of an invention of this magnitude, Father?"

It's his mother who answers, "This will change the course of history to be sure. We just did not think such a thing would be accomplished by *our* son."

Elora slips her hand in his and squeezes.

"And now that you do know?" Duke asks in a tight voice.

The queen studies him, her eyes flashing. "I'm shocked ... and proud. You have accomplished something no one has been able to do. But you cannot abandon your duties to the country as its crown heir. This will be done *if and only if* you have spare time. Is that clear?"

Duke smiles wide, relief coursing through him. "Of course, Mother. It always was."

His mother eyes Elora at his side. "And who is this?"

Duke pulls Elora closer. "She is my chosen bride. You saw her tonight at the masquerade as Lady Elora Thompson."

The queen directs her gaze to Duke. "She looks remarkably like a maid in my employ…who's name is also Elora."

Duke's shoulders tighten.

Your mother doesn't miss a thing.

Char's voice rings unhelpfully in his head. "That's because she *is* your maid, Mother. But now she is to be known as Elora Thompson, from a noble family who live in the Lumiara mountains."

The queen doesn't seem surprised at his words. She studies Elora for several moments.

Elora responds to her appraisal by straightening her spine.

Directing her question to Elora, she asks, "Do you have any idea what it takes to be queen? What makes you think you are up to the task of ruling this country?"

Elora is quiet for a moment before she says in a sure tone. "I have had a strong example to go by, my Queen. You. And with Duke's and, hopefully, your support, I believe I am capable of learning anything I would need to know. I helped Duke build this airplane, so as you can see, I am a good learner."

He smiles inwardly at her spunk in standing up to his indomitable mother. If she is to be his ruling mate one day, she will need it in spades.

"Duke, we will discuss the rest of this back at the palace," his father says, recovering from his surprise.

"I *will* marry Elora. She is my choice," Duke says in an unyielding voice.

The queen continues to watch Elora, who doesn't drop her gaze. His mother says in a tone that resembles steel, "She is clearly very brave and bright to help you build this machine. She'll need to be all those things to survive my court. Are you sure about your choice, Son?"

Duke nods, squeezing Elora's shoulder. "I've never known a finer woman. She reminds me of you, Mother."

The queen's eyes soften at his praise, and she looks between them. "We'll work out the details later."

Huffing in irritation, the king takes one last look at Elora and another scathing one at Char, turns and stomps back to his carriage.

"And your father and I will have to discuss whether that," she points at Char, "will be welcome at the palace."

"She, you mean. Char is a part of me, Mother."

Her shoulders droop, her expression looking tired. "Duke, honestly, give us time to process all this. You've given us much to think upon."

Duke concedes the truth of her words. He nods.

He looks at Char. 'I will never give you up, my friend,' he thinks.

We'll always be together, Prince. Do not fear.

The queen wordlessly follows her husband to the carriage.

Harry laughs, slapping his hands together. "Brother, you sure know how to rile up a nest of hornets. And here's your pet phoenix! Where can I get one?"

Oh, dear heavens. Creator, spare the phoenix who melds with him. She flies off into the night, her tail flickering in agitation over Harry's words.

With a fond look at his brother, Duke watches Char fly away and then takes Elora in both of his arms. He hugs her tightly.

She responds by laughing. "You did it! You told them the truth. I'm so proud of you. And you even told them about our beloved Char!"

He squeezes her to him. "You mean *you* did it, my love. If it wasn't for your reckless, wild plan, this all never would have happened."

She leans back, shrugging. "I had to go to extremes for you to get your due." She searches his eyes. "What happens now?"

"Well," Duke answers, looking around at the growing crowd. The soldiers are now having trouble keeping them back. He trains his gaze on hers. "It seems like we're to have a wedding, Little Spark. That's if, if you're sure you'll have me and the rather hard job of being queen?"

She wraps her arms around his neck, laughing when he leans in and nibbles her ear. "Yes. I'll be your bride, Crown Prince Duke Williams. That's if you dare marry me. You won't be able to expect what I'll do next."

Of which I approve whole-heartedly. Char says from a distance.

He picks Elora up, swinging her around and laughing. "Good. You'll keep me on my toes."

Harry laughs, patting both their backs. "Congratulations to both of you. Don't forget to tell your children that their uncle was the fairy godfather in all of this."

Duke chuckles with Elora as the soldiers lose control of the crowd. They surge toward them, losing their bubble of privacy. They're soon surrounded, but Duke doesn't care who sees when he cups Elora's head in his hands, needing to feel her lips on his more than anything.

She tilts her head, the moonlight illuminating her honey-gold eyes beautifully. They flick to his lips and stay there. Needing no more encouragement, he presses his mouth to hers. Moving his lips against hers, he luxuriates in the softness of her. She responds by kissing him back, but she moans in frustration.

"I'm so short," she complains. "You are too tall to kiss properly." She pouts.

Laughing, he asks, "Is this better?" He sweeps her up in his arms and resumes his kiss of her perfect lips.

She smiles against his mouth and then buries her head in his neck. "Is this real?"

He answers by dipping his head and recapturing her lips with his. Kissing her soundly, he pulls away. "Does that answer your question?"

"Mmmm, maybe you need to show me again."

He doesn't hesitate but does as she asks.

The arrival of a breathless Candy and Lady Elizabeth interrupts their fine moment.

Candy screeches, "Elora Wincham, you *are* in love with the prince! You lied to me!"

Elora grins down at her, nuzzling Duke's throat. "Mmmm, yes, I am. And you have my name wrong. It's Elora Thompson, soon to be Williams. I'm a lady, you know."

Candy coughs. "Yes, I heard all about your rise in society."

Lady Elizabeth clears her throat delicately. "My Prince, would you like some privacy with your, um…"

"Fiancée? Yes, I would," Duke says, not taking his eyes off Elora.

Lady Elizabeth says in a loud voice, "My good people, the prince would like some room."

When only a few pay heed to her words, she's about to call out again when a loud, piercing whistle fills the air.

All heads turn.

Candy stands on the airplane's wing. She holds both her hands, cupping her mouth. "You heard the fine lady. Move! This isn't entertainment for your evening. The Prince wants his space!"

Grumbles sound all around, but between Candy and Lady Elizabeth, they herd the group away to a distance.

"I like a well-spoken woman," Harry comments thoughtfully.

Duke looks between Candy and Lady Elizabeth. "Which one are you referring to?"

Harry smiles, his teeth white and gleaming. "Lady Elizabeth. I've noticed her charms when you didn't. She is quite fetching, I must say."

Duke bumps his brother's shoulder since his hands are so pleasantly occupied. "Well, then, go make a husband of yourself. Talk to the lady."

"I don't mind if I do." He ambles away, stepping directly toward Lady Elizabeth. She turns to him with a smile.

Elora's voice sounds amused. "Now, I didn't see that one coming. But I like it. I like her."

"I do, too. She wasn't right for me, but she would make an excellent princess for Harry."

Elora leans back in his arms. "Now that I have you alone, what about my money?"

Duke nudges her nose with his. "How about I pay it off slowly? Give me another fifty years?"

"No," she says. "The bargain needs to be fulfilled, or I can't talk about your secret life. I'd like to have the use of my hand, thank you very much."

"I believe the bargain specifically says, you cannot talk of my proclivities. Well, now that everyone knows about the airplane, it's not so secret."

Her eyes flash. "Do you have more secrets I'll find out about later, Prince? Are you saying you'll continue to have proclivities?"

He laughs. "No, but I might. I haven't thought of any yet."

"Well, just in case. Pay me, Prince." She adds to her statement by pressing soft kisses to his neck.

Enjoying the feel of her lips, he'd agree to anything. "Fine, I'll pay you as soon as we get to the palace. I'll raid the treasury for the exorbitant sum I owe you."

"No," she says again, pouting. "First, you will return to kissing me. Then, we'll go."

He can only obey her wishes, thinking all of his have come true. With her lips on his, life is very sweet indeed.

Epilogue

The Nebraria Gazette

*T*he land of Nebraria, in the year 1848, held a coronation, crowning the new King Harry Williams and his bride, the Lady Elizabeth Strafford, Queen of all fae lands.

The land has finally recovered from the previous year's scandal. When the former king, in a move that surprised all of Nebraria, abdicated his throne to the younger prince instead of the eldest, Duke, it left the country reeling.

Apparently, Duke's actions as a secret inventor and marrying a former maid in the palace were punishable enough to make him lose his crown. The palace tried to keep the former Elora Wincham's identity a secret, but word spread quickly after her historic flight over the Midnight Ball as to who she truly is.

The former prince heir has handled the transition very well, focusing all of his attention on the building of an airplane factory he built two leagues to the west. Aspiring engineers are to continue to apply to the palace office for a chance to work on the crew.

The Gazette is happy to report the latest news. King Harry's wedding to Lady Elizabeth last year has already produced results! Along with the coronation, there is the joyful news that the King and Queen are expecting an heir. Nebraria waits with hope for news of a healthy child.

The King has started his reign lifting the ban on phoenixes as he has, along with his brother, mind-melded with the fierce creature. This marks a new era of bonds with the elusive birds and fae across the land are looking for nests to encourage new bonds.

A former palace manservant, now engineer, Grant Boswell, has this to say about the new King. "With the many new changes King Harry is implementing, we can trust he is leading Nebraria into a promising new age."

The End

This book was an absolute joy to write. It is one that I can read over and over and never tire of it. The *story* was just so much fun. And it has my all-time favorite character I've ever written, Char, the phoenix. She is sass at its finest, snark divine.

I'd also like to note that I did my best when I wrote the mechanics inside and out of the first airplane. I do know it's not completely right, I used creative license to build the engine, start it and make that first historic flight. I'd like to thank Jake Stoddard, my beta reader/editor for his meticulous notes on his understanding of how a plane works. I had some things right, but many wrong. Thanks to him, this is somewhat correct.

Fun fact about this book: I ate an entire 3 pound 4 ounce bag of gummy worms editing this fine story, maybe it's sweetness rubbed off?

I'm also including the playlist I listened to while writing, I always like to peek inside an author's mind and see what inspired them to write the story:

Laisse tomber les filles by Annie Trousseau
Sounds Like Something I'd Do by Drake Milligan
War Cry by Band Jaren
That's Life by Frank Sinatra
Once Upon a December by Christy Altomare
You're the One That I Want by John Travolta and Olivia New-

ton-John
Stop and Stare by OneRepublic
Shut Up and Dance by WALK THE MOON
Sweet Caroline by Neil Diamond
I'm Gonne Be (500 Miles) by The Proclaimers
I Think They Call This Love by Elliot James Reay
Ave Maria by Dimash Qudaibergen
Non, je ne regrette rien by Edith Piaf
Fairytale by Alexander Rybak
Le vent, le cri by HAUSER, London Symphany Orchestra
Photograph/Claire de Lune by Cody Fry
Beautiful Things by Benson Boone
golden hour by JVKE
Snowman by Sia

N
W
E
S
LURIN
THORNVEIL ISLE
AKININIA
NEBRARIA
BOER
LUMIARA MOUNTAINS
ROSEMERE
OCEANEA
SANDOVAL
EKLOS

For fans of adventurous fantasy with clean romance comes Realms of Lurin, a multi-author collection of standalone regency-inspired fantasy novellas featuring different magical creatures and taking place in the same world.

Be sure to check out all the books in the Realms of Lurin Series.

Sirens and Sea Captains by Courtney Denelsbeck

Petals and Poison by Cara Ruegg

Venom and Vows by Maegwen Salley-Massie

Fae and Flames by Sofia Simpson

Goblins and Crystals by C.A. Meadows

Witches and Wolves by Nellie Peters

Tempest and Tiger's Eye by Gabriella Batel

Beaux and Dragons by Candice Pedraza Yamnitz

Acknowledgements

To my God, I give Him thanks every day and pray every morning that He is Who I look to for every story and that He might be praised in them.

Also, my husband. Without his support, I could not write and certainly not full-time. He's my inspiration for every romance and I love how he reminds me every day that true love is real.

This novella could not have been done without the invitation to join seven other lovely ladies to write in the world of Lurin. I thank Maegwen Salley-Massie for her invite and for Courtney Denelsbeck for her idea to put this all together.

As for the story itself, I have to thank Maegwen Salley-Massie and CA Meadows for their constant support and encouragement as the story unfolded.

This also would not be the story it is without the talents of my developmental editor, Jessica Gwyn and beta reader extraordinaire, Jake Stoddard. Their input was invaluable and if you enjoyed the story, they had a huge part in making it what it is. Jessica, as always, has a way of tightening my sentences and giving insight I never would have thought of. Jake is the reason the historic flight was possible in this story. Did I know what yaw was before his intervention? No, I did not. Plus, there were many other instances that wouldn't make sense without his input. He didn't let me get away with anything! Good thing.

Thank you to my dear friends, Dana, Jenny and Darcy for your open ears on hearing every detail behind the scenes of writing a story.

And to my readers, thank you for reading my books. I write for you and for you to have a chance to read a good romance without the steam. This was truly my favorite book to write... I hope you enjoyed it.

S ofia grew up moving constantly. Never in one place more than three years, there was plenty of time to daydream and wish for better stories than what her life offered.

Books were an escape from tragedy after tragedy. Jesus was an ever-present comfort to her, gifting her with His peace when she so desperately needed it.

College finally gave her a chance to study what she had always dreamed of doing, writing her stories. She obtained a B.A. in Journalism, married her handsome husband and had two amazing sons.

She's also the proud mother of a fluffy-not-fat cat and a 100-pound Doberman who loves his momma's lap.

A big believer in dreaming big, Sofia loves speaking to youth, encouraging them to find hope no matter what their life looks like. She also plans and hosts teen balls where every teen leaves with a clean book. Sofia is a daughter of the Lord first and foremost and finds inspiration with the stories like King David, Ruth, and Esther.

www.ingramcontent.com/pod-product-compliance
Lightning Source LLC
Chambersburg PA
CBHW031038160726
47991CB00005B/1941